I0679385

Nine Brides for Cowboy Creek

Volume 4
Scarlett & Rachael

by

Teresa Slack

Other Titles

Nine Brides for Cowboy Creek

Rennie
Eliza
Carrie
Bridget
Katie
Marianne
Scarlett
Rachael
Amelia

Four Sisters Ranch

Priscilla's Promise

Willow Wood Brides Series

A Promise for Josie—
Available free to newsletter subscribers
A Lawman for Lisette
A Love Letter for Jessa
A Dream for Harper
A Wedding for Felicity
A Hero for Ellie
A Cowboy for Meggan

Jenna's Creek Series:

Streams of Mercy
Redemption's Song
Evidence of Grace
A Jenna's Creek Wedding: *A Christmas Novella*
Legacy of Faith
Tender Blessings Series:
Love Begins
A Little Goodbye

Stand Alone Novels

The Ultimate Guide to Darcy Carter
Runaway Heart
Joy Redefined
Cheater, Cheater: Lindsay's Turn

What Readers are Saying

"Teresa Slack is a one-click author for me!!"

"Compelling story with fun new slant on the mail-order bride genre."

"Just keeps getting better! I love each story the brides bring to this series! How God always uses whatever path we take and brings His design full circle. Can't wait for the next book!"

"A must read for those who enjoy Historical Christian books… from a delightful author."

"Outstanding series will have you binge reading!"

"A quick read without any drawn-out contrivances to belabor the crisis before the happy ending. Should not be missed. Want to see more of these characters. Good job, Ms. Slack!"

"Extremely well-written, tender story of great disappointment and pain before eventually finding their way to an honest and beautiful love. I highly recommend this wonderfully written story."

"Slack has done it again. This book did not disappoint! I read it in one afternoon. So good I can hardly wait to read the next one!"

"I loved the hero. He was not typical or handsome by the world's standards but by the ones that matter. I read this over twice. Enjoyed this story very much."

"...Loved this book. Teresa's characters are interesting and real. This book hooked me in the first pages. I can hardly wait until the next book comes out."

"...Intense action and tender moments to warm your heart. Well written...and the ending wrapped everything up nicely. I highly recommend reading it." –

"A good balance of action, life in the West, danger and romance. The characters were well developed, and the settings described so well that the reader feels right there."

"Another wonderful read... These kinds of stories keep you intrigued, wondering how the love story will pan out."

"A story of forgiveness, new relationships, new love, accepting yourself and moving on."

"Rating this book a 5! ...Teresa's work never fails to keep me on my toes from beginning to end. I would love to read the next book in the series, or even one of the author's previous series. Never disappointed."

For Ralph. With Love. Always.

Nine Brides for Cowboy Creek Book 7

Scarlett

TERESA SLACK

Chapter One

Scarlett Sanders clasped her hands in her lap and swallowed the lump in her throat. Not that long ago she was breathing poisonous fumes and coughing her lungs away in an airless laundry in Cincinnati. Back then, she didn't waste time or energy wondering if something better was in store for her than the backbreaking tedium of washing and mending rugs, curtains, and bedding for hotels. Today she sat in a drafty meetinghouse that served as a church to watch her sister marry the man who had saved them from a kidnapping ring.

She would've pinched herself to make sure she wasn't dreaming had she not worried her new neighbors would see her and think she was off in the head. She had often wondered the same thing after letting Marianne talk her into coming to Cowboy Creek to find husbands among a group of lonely ranchers.

It couldn't have worked out better for Marianne. It was obvious from the look on her flushed face that she was crazy in love with her ginger-haired cowboy. Scarlett smiled to herself as she remembered how hard Marianne tried to convince Scarlett and herself that Nathan Lake was too reserved and stoic for her. And oh, how stubborn! Something the tenacious Marianne couldn't abide in other people. She might've thought she could trick herself into believing Nathan wasn't the man for her, but she could never fool Scarlett.

As if sensing her gaze, Marianne looked away from the preacher at the front of the room and her groom, who kept tugging at the collar of his shirt, and gave Scarlett a smile of unadulterated contentment.

Scarlett nearly burst into tears of joy. Marianne spent most of her life working and sacrificing to make things better for them that she seldom took a minute to consider her own needs and wants. When they were little, the sisters would snuggle in the bed they shared and imagine the strong, handsome men they would someday marry. The places they would live and the children they would have. Scarlett pictured four boys and four girls for herself and spent those nights deciding on names for them. Marianne always laughed and said Scarlett would get nothing done but growing beans to feed them all and sewing patches on their clothes. Marianne said she didn't care how many children she had as long as their pa was tall and handsome and brave, and he stuck around to take care of them. And that they grew up playing and learning and laughing with Scarlett's brood of eight.

With the adoring Nathan beside her, Marianne would never have to worry about what her children would eat or if there'd be coal for the stove the way she and Scarlett had done those long-ago nights.

The sisters exchanged tearful smiles before Marianne turned back to her groom. After they repeated their vows, she would ride to Nathan's farm and begin a completely new life as a frontier wife.

Without Scarlett.

Scarlett swallowed a lump of melancholy laced with a healthy dash of trepidation. What did these wonderful changes in Marianne's life mean for Scarlett? What would her new life look like? Life without Marianne would be scary and overwhelming enough in the city. What in the world could she expect from it in this remote community without a friend to her name?

There were two unattached men left in Cowboy Creek who wanted brides. She stole a quick peek over her right shoulder. Travis Lindell was looking straight at her. Her cheeks flushed, and she quickly faced forward. This wasn't the first time since she walked into the meetinghouse that she caught Travis watching her. She wouldn't let her pride get inflated. Any woman would get noticed in this crowd.

There was no denying Travis was handsome. He looked close to six feet tall. He had wide shoulders, a chest as big around as an oak tree, and narrow hips. His chiseled features would draw attention in any setting. His expressive golden-brown eyes, the color of cinnamon, and an engaging smile could melt the chilliest woman's heart. In Scarlett's experience a handsome face and confident bearing were no indication of moral character or a good heart. She'd encountered plenty of good-looking, smooth-talking men in her life who weren't worth their weight in salt. Something about Travis told her he wasn't like that. He was authentic.

Next to Travis sat the blacksmith. Shorter than Travis by a couple of inches, Lonnie Fanshaw was a large man with hands the size of ham-hocks. If looks were any indication, he was the oldest man in the group. Scarlett was twenty-three and hoped to find a husband closer to her own age. Lonnie didn't have Travis's chiseled good looks either, but he had a warm smile and twinkling eyes that suggested intelligence and a quick wit.

The only other man without a woman on his arm was Rase Canfield, the apparent leader of the group. Marla Dodds, the preacher's wife, told Scarlett he had no interest in a bride. Marla believed if the parade of lovely women who had moved to Cowboy Creek since January didn't change Rase's mind about getting married, nothing would. Once he realized how happy and contented and well-fed the other men were, he'd want a wife of his own.

"Some men take longer than others to recognize life's better with a wife," Marla had finished with a knowing smile.

Scarlett wasn't interested in converting a confirmed bachelor. She wasn't convinced any of the men in the group was the husband for her. Coming here was Marianne's dream. Scarlett had come because that was how she responded to all Marianne's ideas. She trusted her sister, despite the mountain of doubt weighing on her when they left Cincinnati.

She wouldn't encourage Travis too soon, no matter how attractive. Lassoing a man wasn't in the forefront of her mind. She was too relieved to be out of the industrial laundry and out of the sick bed where she'd been convalescing. For now, she'd focus on the good things that had happened the last few weeks. She had been rescued from a kidnapping ring. Marianne was marrying the man she loved. The air in Cowboy Creek was sweet and clean and a balm to Scarlett's weary soul and body. The people were kind and welcoming. She couldn't think of a better place to complete her recovery.

When the preacher's last Amen signaled the end of the ceremony, conversation, punctuated by chairs and boots scraping the worn wooden floor, filled the old building. Scarlett left her seat and hurried to Marianne before the other women could surround her with well wishes. The sisters embraced. "Oh, Marianne. You've got love written all over you. I'm so happy for you."

When Marianne pulled away, tears shone in her brown eyes. Marianne had always been strong and practical. It was jarring for Scarlett to see her looking so in love. Vulnerable. Carefree. "I'm so glad you're here, Scarlett. This day wouldn't have been the same without you."

Marianne's new husband enveloped Scarlett's hands in his. "I'm honored to have you here, Scarlett, and glad you finally made it to Cowboy Creek."

"Thank you, Mr. Lake."

He chuckled and squeezed her hand. "None of that. It's Nathan. We're family."

Family.

It had been so long since Scarlett and Marianne had anyone besides each other, the concept would take some getting used to. As the other women crowded in around the new couple to kiss Marianne and offer their congratulations, the room quickly emptied of chairs. The men were carrying everything outside so the group could share the wedding feast in the glorious late summer sunshine.

Scarlett let herself be swept along with the others to waiting wagons and horses where the women unloaded boxes, crocks wrapped in towels, and canvas bags from wagon beds or from saddlebags.

A warm breeze belied the chill of an approaching autumn. Splashes of yellow in the trees were the only precursor anyone was willing to recognize before winter descended on their valley. This morning as Scarlett and Marianne had laughed and teased over warm bread pudding to honor Marianne's last breakfast as an unmarried woman, Marla told them Marianne wouldn't have long to enjoy her new husband. Harvest was starting soon. In another week or so, no one in Cowboy Creek would have a moment to exhale amidst the added chores as they prepared for winter.

Scarlett went to the nearest rig where a tall, thin woman was taking a stack of blankets out of the back. "Need any help?"

The woman smiled. "Sure. Do you care to spread these on the tables?" She handed the stack to Scarlett. "I'm Bridget DeSantis. You're Marianne's sister, yes?"

Scarlett returned her smile. "I'm Scarlett Sanders."

"Well, we sure are glad to have you, Scarlett. We're nearly full up on brides. Soon all the men who want wives will have one. We hope." She hefted a box loaded with plates and silverware from the sounds of it into her long arms. They walked side by side to where the men were placing chairs around a table fashioned from planks of lumber set over sawhorses.

Scarlett waited for a man to set a chair in place and move out of the way so she could throw a blanket over.

Travis Lindell came up beside her and touched the brim of his hat. "Miss Scarlett." He took hold of a corner of the blanket. "Allow me." Holding onto his end, he circled the table and smoothed it over the rough lumber. Scarlett unfurled the others, tossing an end to Travis. In no time the long table was covered. Travis kept his eyes on her as they worked, an infectious smile in place.

She blushed furiously, wishing his attention didn't make her feel like a silly schoolgirl. She marveled that he hadn't been snatched up by another bride before now. "You act like you've done that before," she said when he circled the table back to her side.

"I've set a table a time or two in my time."

"I can see that."

"Would it be all right if I sat next to you while we eat?"

Scarlett's blush deepened. She cast her gaze away. She wasn't sure how this operation worked. Had Travis just laid claim to her? Was she obligated to pair up with him because he worked faster than the others? She had planned to sit next to Marianne. Marianne's attention was rightly focused on Nathan. Scarlett didn't want to intrude, but she was completely unsettled without Marianne's reassuring presence. Those easy days were over. It was time she figured out what she wanted and how to get it without relying on her big sister. The only way to find out if she was compatible with the handsome cowboy was to get to know him. "I'd like that, Mr. Lindell."

Warmth lit up his lively brown eyes. "I'd feel better if you called me Travis."

"Then I will, and you must call me Scarlett."

He touched the brim of his hat again and walked back toward the meetinghouse. Scarlett tried not to stare after him. That was unladylike, though nature sure had made it hard not to take a second look. She smoothed her hands over her skirt and turned back to the tables.

A woman with tawny brown hair and serious hazel eyes was setting out plates and forks from a basket. She stopped in her duties long enough to place a hand on the small of her back. She winced as she stretched. Scarlett glanced around the gathering of women. Even the slender Bridget bore a widening of her hips that suggested a baby was on the way. It was to be expected. There was no way to prevent babies once a preacher blessed a union. She heard talk aplenty in the factories of tonics and potions and methods to delay the inevitable. As far as she knew, babies came when the Lord willed, and neither man nor beast could stop it.

It didn't look like the women of Cowboy Creek were interested in delaying anything. By this time next year, every husband in the group would be eating a lot of burnt suppers as babies took over the household schedules.

She went to the woman with the basket. "Could I help?"

The tawny-haired woman gratefully handed over the basket. She gingerly twisted her back. "Got a catch in my back. It's gotten so I can't get a good night's sleep."

Bridget looked up from cutting cubes of cornbread and arranging them in a basket. "Eliza, you've probably had the last good night's sleep you're going to get. I'd say for the next fifteen years." She winked at Scarlett.

Eliza caught the wink. "Looks like I'm not the only one, Bridget DeSantis. I'm Eliza Waring," she said to Scarlett. "Over there's my husband Adam." She wagged her chin in the direction of the only man dressed in a neat black suit. Even the preacher wasn't as smartly attired. "We live half a mile northeast of the trading post. Stop over and see us anytime. You might have to hunt us down in the fields or at the creek, but there's usually a cake or a pie cooling on the sideboard and I'd love to share a piece with you."

"Thank you, Mrs.—"

"Just Eliza."

"Be sure to take your work gloves," Bridget said playfully. "Eliza will find a job for you. No grass grows under this one."

Eliza glared, but Scarlett saw a teasing gleam in her eyes. "What's wrong with that? Winter will be upon us soon enough with nothing to do but sit around." She shuddered. "I can't abide sitting around."

"Once that baby gets here, you won't have to worry about nothing to do." Bridget looked at Scarlett. "You should see the Waring place. Eliza whitewashed the whole thing herself. Can you imagine? I never thought I'd see a whitewashed house after I left home. Dominic and I will have to do the same thing with our new house. Can't let the Warings get one over on us. Now, she's putting a fence all the way around the yard, probably in preparation for the little one, and it's whitewashed too."

Eliza nudged Scarlett with her elbow hard enough to nearly push her into the table. "Listen to her. That poor husband of hers is building a showplace big enough for ten children on their ridge. On a clear day you can practically see it from Good Hope. And she's after me about whitewash."

A young woman with glossy black hair and snapping dark eyes set a kettle on the table at Scarlett's elbow. "Don't let their bickering fool you. They're best friends, though you can barely tell it most days." She smoothed a stray wisp of hair away from her forehead. "Scarlett, right? You look just like your sister. I'm Katie Jamison."

Scarlett gasped. "Katie." She hugged the other woman, then pulled back, embarrassed. "I'm sorry. Marianne's talked about you so much, I feel like I've known you for ages."

Katie laughed and hugged her back. "No need to apologize. I always wanted a sister. Now I feel like I have five. With you here, it makes six. Welcome to Cowboy Creek."

Chapter Two

Familiar feminine laughter drew Scarlett's attention to the other side of the yard. Marianne's hand rested possessively on Nathan's arm. He covered her hand with his and squeezed, pulling her against him. They shared an intimate smile and a word meant only for each other's ears.

Next to Scarlett, Katie sighed. "I've never seen your sister so lighthearted and peaceful. She's like a different person."

Scarlett kept her eyes on Marianne. "It's a long way from Cincinnati. She looks like a girl again." Tears clogged the back of her throat.

Katie lifted the lid from the pot she'd set on the table and stirred with a long ladle. The aroma of cooked meat and vegetables teased Scarlett's palate. She was thankful to have her appetite back after losing so much weight over the last few months.

"If anyone deserves happiness, it's Marianne," Katie said. "She was such a good friend to me at the Winninghams. So generous. Always willing to help another of us girls out."

Scarlett murmured her agreement. Loyal and selfless—the best words to describe Marianne. As though sensing her gaze, Marianne looked over. It had always been that way—like they could read each other's thoughts without words. They exchanged a look until Nathan said something, and Marianne turned back to him.

Scarlett's heart lurched. She needed to tell Marianne what Dr. Gaetz had said the last time she saw him. If not, Marianne would figure it out just by looking into her eyes. Then she would be mad Scarlett tried to keep something from her. Just not today. Today she wouldn't dream of spoiling her sister's happiness by giving her something to worry about. Something that may never happen or wouldn't change by fretting over it.

Travis approached carrying a chair under each arm. He placed them side by side. A smile curved his lips as he glanced at Scarlett before going back inside the meetinghouse.

"It looks like someone has noticed you," Bridget said.

Scarlett was thankful for something to think about besides Dr. Gaetz's prognosis, though she wasn't much more comfortable thinking about Travis. She wasn't sure she wanted to invest time into a relationship she might never be able to cultivate.

Eliza handed Bridget two jars of pickles across the table. "Of course she has. She's young enough and pretty enough. Travis has been waiting nine months for a bride. Longer than that, I'm sure." She looked at Scarlett. "He has a ranch about three miles from here. Plenty of open land he hasn't had a chance to tend. Too much work for one man on his own. That's what all our men faced before we brides arrived. More than enough potential but not enough manpower to do the work. Don't let Travis's easy-going attitude fool you. He's proud and a hard worker. He'll give anything for this land."

"Like all the men in Cowboy Creek," Bridget put in. "This is a hard life. I grew up in a big house on the river with housemaids and doting parents." Her smile softened. "I miss my parents every day. Sometimes I even miss the city. But I feel like I didn't start living until I came here. You might find it's the same for you."

Peace and contentment shone on the other women's faces. Scarlett envied them. They knew what they wanted when they came here. Escape or security or the freedom to make their own choices. Whatever their hopes and goals, it looked like they found them. Marianne too. Now it was up to Scarlett to figure out what she wanted and if this was the place in which to find it.

When the last chair was set in place, everyone gathered around the table. Preach and Marla sat at the head of the table with Nathan and Marianne next to them. Travis pulled a chair away from the table and motioned Scarlett into it.

She smiled her thanks and sat down. A dark-headed girl with cherubic features climbed into the chair next to her. "I'm Annie," her little voice piped. "I'm five years old. Almost six, Mama says."

Scarlett smiled apologetically at Travis over the child's head. He cocked an eyebrow in defeat and claimed the next chair. After a brief prayer from Preach and a blessing for the newly married couple, everyone dug in. While Annie chattered between bites, Scarlett and Travis exchanged smiles.

"I understand you and your sister heard about Cowboy Creek through Katie," Travis managed when Annie stopped talking long enough to chew.

"She and Marianne worked for the same family in Cincinnati," she replied. "I didn't meet her until today."

They both watched Katie with her new husband for a moment. "I don't know her very well myself," Travis said. "She's quiet, like Sawyer. I guess that's why they're a good match. Sawyer's more outspoken now that Katie's here. Kept to himself before. Only good friend he had was Nathan. Now he opens up to 'bout everybody. Does the neighborly thing before anyone has to ask. I guess that's what a good woman does—brings out the best in a man." Longing darkened his cinnamon-brown eyes.

Annie spared Scarlett from responding by launching into a story of finding a wriggling cocoon of bagworms attached to a tree by the creek a few months earlier. "Papa tore it open, and worms fell all over the ground." She wrinkled her nose in disgust. "He said some years there's a lot of bags of worms and they can kill the trees they hang onto."

"Annie, don't talk about things like that at the table," said a girl about thirteen from the other side of the table.

"I'm just telling them what Papa said," Annie retorted. She looked solemnly at Scarlett. "That's my sister Candace. She thinks she's the boss of me. She's really not."

Scarlett bit back a smile. She pointed at Marianne. "And that's my sister. She always thought she was the boss of me. She loves me, and I'm glad I have her. She took care of me since I was a girl no bigger than you."

"Who will take care of you now?"

Scarlett's gaze flitted to Travis, embarrassed. He had leaned in and looked as anxious for an answer as Annie. "I'm grown now. I can take care of myself, with God's help of course."

Annie drew back, her eyes wide. "Not me. I'd be too scared to take care of myself. I'm never gonna grow up. I'm gonna live with Mama and Papa forever."

Scarlett didn't tell her she was nearly as scared.

After dinner, the men clustered around the hitching rail pulling on pipes and talking and laughing while the women gathered the leftover food and did their own share of gossiping and discussing of the coming week. They piled plates with food for the newlyweds to take home so Marianne wouldn't have to fool with cooking for a day or two. The men clapped Nathan on the back and offered good-natured advice, not that any of them besides Preach knew more about being a husband than Nathan did. It looked to Scarlett like a learn-as-you-go endeavor.

Marianne broke away from the women and drew Scarlett aside. Despite her joy for Marianne, Scarlett couldn't hold back her tears. Marianne was only fifteen months older than she was, but she had always seemed so much more mature. So much wiser and braver. No matter how sullen Ma and Pa became when they were drinking or how much they fought, no matter how often they lost jobs or forgot to bring food home, Scarlett always knew, no matter what, she could count on Marianne. Her sister was now Nathan's wife. Soon enough, she would be somebody's mother. She wouldn't have time to be Scarlett's sister.

Marianne pulled her into her arms. "We haven't had a moment to talk all day. I want to hear what Doc Gaetz said. How are you? Your color's better." She laid her hand on Scarlett's cheek and studied her face. "You still look weak. You've lost so much weight. What did he say about that?"

Scarlett laughed and pulled away. "Stop fussing, will you? I'm fine. You're the one about to ride into the country to become a farmer's wife. You need all your strength for that."

Marianne wasn't fooled. "I hate leaving when we haven't had time to talk." She looked over her shoulder where Nathan waited next to the wagon. "Come out to the ranch tomorrow. Marla can ride with you and show you the way."

Scarlett laughed again. "I'm sure I'm the last person Nathan wants to see tomorrow. You two will want to spend some time alone."

Marianne blushed again. Scarlett liked her independent sister's new, softer look. "I suppose. But we need to talk. All we've had time for the last few days is getting ready for today. I want to know how long the doctor thinks you need to recuperate. Does he know how sick you were before we left Cincinnati? I'm sure you told him about the chemicals in that laundry. Did you tell him how the other girls—"

"Marianne, stop. You know as well as I do everyone recuperates at their own rate. He said the best thing for me is fresh air. The same thing you've been saying for years." Scarlett gave her a quick hug. "I don't want you to worry one more minute about me. Your husband is getting impatient."

Marianne glanced over her shoulder and exchanged a look with Nathan. When she turned back to Scarlett, she looked flustered, something else Scarlett wasn't used to seeing from her generally unruffled sister. "I saw you talking with Travis Lindell. Isn't he handsome? Not as handsome as Nathan, but—"

"Marianne! We're not worrying about me. Nathan's waiting. Go!"

The sisters laughed again and kissed each other. Scarlett was startled to feel Marianne trembling. Whether from excitement, anxiety, happiness, or a combination of the three, she couldn't tell. She'd love to know how Marianne was feeling right now—her concerns, thoughts, fears—but there was no time. Their lives had changed, and there was no going back. They broke apart. Scarlett joined the other women, waving and smiling as the newlyweds climbed into the wagon and drove away.

She blinked against the plume of dirt and grit in the wake of the wagon and hoped it provided a good excuse for her red eyes. Loneliness and near panic washed over her. With the stroke of a pen, her sister had become Marianne Lake.

Who was she now?

Chapter Three

"She's not that far away."

Scarlett had gotten so lost in her thoughts, she hadn't noticed Travis walk up to her.

She looked around the emptying churchyard. "I'm sorry?"

"Your sister." He wagged his head in the direction the wagon had taken. "Nathan's place—her place, too—is just a short buggy ride down the road. Faster on horseback."

She sighed. "I know. I was just thinking..."

"About how everything's changed so fast you can barely keep up?"

She gave him a small smile. "Exactly."

He nodded and turned his attention back down the road where the sound of Nathan's wagon had been absorbed into the night. A breeze kicked up, carrying a hint of rain. Scarlett tightened her shawl around her, though the temperature was still pleasant, and faced the horizon.

Travis looped his thumbs in his belt and rocked back on his heels. "It's changed a lot for us too. Wasn't that long ago it was just Preach and Marla and a few lonely cowboys and out-of-work miners trying to make a go of things. Now we got women's voices singing in church. A lot better grub at Sunday meetings. And young'uns talking about bagworms at the table."

Scarlett laughed. "I'm sure her mother won't be too happy to hear it."

"I won't tell if you don't." His smile widened. It was certainly a charming smile. Scarlett could barely look away. "Church meeting was about the only time any of us got together," he went on. "Plenty of weeks I didn't see another face between Sundays. Only other voice I heard was my horse."

The churchyard was quiet. Marla and Preach had gone into their apartment in the back of the trading post. Two men—Rase and Lonnie, Scarlett thought, though it was hard to tell in the gathering darkness—were carrying the last of the sheets of lumber used for the tables back into the meetinghouse. From down the road came the voices of the Whitamore children as they walked home. The creek whispered its song on the other side of the barn.

A gust of wind rushed down the street, stirring a smattering of dried leaves around their feet. Travis held his hat in place until it passed. The silence of the evening pressed in. No hucksters hawked their wares. No music and raucous laughter spilled out of the bawdy houses. No din of grinding machinery from the factories. No boat whistles blasting off the river. No barking dogs or voices calling inside the tenements. Even the Whitamore children's voices had gone quiet.

"A person could find this quite…isolating," she said. "What made you settle here?"

"Wasn't nowhere else calling my name," he said simply after taking a few moments to formulate an answer.

Scarlett expected him to say he came for the open space. The opportunity to build something of his own. Freedom. "There's a lot of places to go for a man looking for opportunity."

His gaze traveled toward the distant mountains. "Not for me. As soon as I saw this place, I knew it was what I wanted. I don't have any family tying me to a certain place. My mama died when I was a boy. Wasn't nobody else, leastways not that I know of. Town wasn't for me. I didn't like people hemming me, using up all the air. What about you? What made you and Marianne come?"

She thought about giving him a pat answer, something he expected to hear about how women didn't have choices in the city. If one wasn't born into a comfortable life or didn't marry young, there weren't a lot of options open to her. He already knew all that.

"We wanted something different too. Marianne did, anyway. After she heard about Cowboy Creek from Katie, she couldn't think on anything else. Once Marianne gets a notion in her head, there's no dislodging it. She figured we needed out of the city, and Cowboy Creek sounded perfect to her."

"And what about you? What did you want?"

She wouldn't tell him she'd been thinking on that exact thing all day. She hadn't given her dreams and desires much thought since she was a girl. Surviving had taken up all her energy. It had seemed so simple when she and Marianne lay in bed and daydreamed about husbands and babies and houses. Then life happened and the immediate need for food and clothing and shoes without holes took the place of girlish wishes.

Another gust of air careened down the street, raising a cloud of dust. It stirred the tail of her skirt and the hem of her shawl. She and Travis lowered their heads and squinted against it.

The familiar tickle of a cough started in the back of her throat, benign and inconvenient. She hoped it stayed that way. She delicately cleared her throat behind her handkerchief. "I suppose I want the same as everyone. For my sister to be happy and healthy. That's in Nathan's hands now."

She sighed wistfully. She wanted to say more, but the cough was building. She cleared her throat again, stronger this time. She looked away. She didn't want Travis to see the widening of her eyes as her lungs tried to expand against the tightening in her chest. She tried to moisten the inside of her mouth.

What had he asked her? She couldn't remember. All she could think of was filling her lungs with sweet oxygen. "It's getting late. I should..." She pressed the handkerchief to her lips.

Frown lines appeared between Travis's eyes. "Scarlett?"

The cough erupted. Scarlett buried her face in her shawl. She hated him to see her like this, but there was nothing to be done to stop it now. Travis put out his hand as if to pat her back. He must've recognized the futility of such a move. "I'll be right back," he murmured and hurried away.

Knowing there was no delicate way to placate the cough, Scarlett put her hands on her knees and let it have its way. By the time Travis rushed back with a tin cup of water, her face flamed from exertion and embarrassment.

Travis put a hand on her elbow and steered her to a hitching rail. Scarlett leaned against it and took a cautious sip of water. The coughing eased. She sipped from the cup until the fit passed and the cup was empty. She stared into the cup as she dabbed her chin with her dress sleeve.

"I'm…sorry…"

Travis cut off the apology, his face dark with concern. "Are you going to be all right? Should I fetch Marla? Or go for Marianne?"

"No! Please. Don't do that." She took a few slow breaths. "I'm…I'm all right."

"You don't look all right. You look…"

Scarlett was glad he didn't finish. She already knew. She looked sickly. Weak. Pathetic.

"I'm all right. I promise. I just need…to rest." Her hands shook. She set the cup on the hitching rail and hid her hands in the folds of her skirt.

Travis eased onto the hitching rail beside her as if afraid a sudden movement would incite another spell. "That was…worrisome. Does it happen often?"

Scarlett smoothed her hair back from her face and fluffed her sleeves to give her breathing time to slow down. She didn't want him to realize the severity of the situation. Or worse, tell Marianne. When and if it became necessary for Marianne to know how sick she was, Scarlett would do the telling. In the meantime, she didn't want anyone worrying or feeling sorry for her.

"Back home, I worked in an industrial laundry where I breathed in dangerous chemicals all day. Before that I worked at a clothing factory. We sewed pockets into men's trousers. It was heavy work. By the end of the day, my back and shoulders ached from forcing the fabric through the machines. The worst thing was the tiny fibers floating in the air. No matter how loud those machines thumped, you could hear girls coughing up and down the lines. Sometimes, someone would stop working to cough up a ball of lint. The foremen always yelled and threatened to dock our pay until we got back to work."

Travis sucked air between his teeth. "Hard way to make a living."

"Today the dirt in the wind got the cough going. It happens that way sometimes. I haven't coughed like that since I left Dr. Gaetz's house. It's getting better."

Travis motioned to the bench on the narrow trading post porch and offered his elbow. Scarlett hoped he wouldn't notice the trembling in her knees as they stepped onto the porch. The heat slowly left her face, and her breathing eased.

"What about you?" she asked after they were settled. "What did you do before you came here?"

"I was thirteen when I struck out on my own."

"Thirteen? I can't imagine." Thirteen and alone. Her life had been hard, but at least she had Marianne.

"Mama had been gone four or five years by then. I'd been living off the charity of others since she died. Before that, actually. I worked as a stable hand for Mr. Keplinger, her boss. It was a decent enough job for a boy but not for a man."

"But thirteen. That's not a man. Weren't you scared?"

"More than you know, but I knew I couldn't stay where I was. Nothing good was going to come to me as long as I hung around there."

"So you came here?"

"Eventually. I punched cattle off and on. Took odd jobs wherever I could find them. Sometimes worked for nothing more than a bowl of beans and a warm hay mow to throw my bedroll. It wasn't so bad. There are plenty who've had it worse. I picked up a lot of skills along the way. I knew God was with me, almost like He was leading me from place to place, job to job. Keeping me safe. Teaching me. It was hard, lean times, but it made me who I am. I couldn't run my place on my own now if I hadn't learned what I did during that time."

They sat side by side, staring into the empty path that constituted Cowboy Creek's only street. Behind them, Scarlett heard the soft murmurs of Preach and Marla's voices inside their living quarters. The cadence was peaceful. Soothing. She always wondered what married people talked about at the end of a hard day of building a life together.

Her parents never talked. They shouted. Bickered. Drank and hurled insults. Laughed too loud at things that weren't funny. When they finally kicked her and Marianne out of the house for the last time, Scarlett was almost relieved. Like Travis, she had been scared but knew nothing good would come of staying with them. Without their angry voices bouncing off her chest, a huge weight was lifted.

"I have a lot of chores at home before I turn in." Travis's voice was heavy with reluctance.

"Oh, yes, I..." For the first time in her life, she didn't have an endless list of chores waiting, except to help Marla in the morning with whatever she wanted done. "I shouldn't have kept you so long."

He pulled in his long legs and stood. Scarlett tightened her shawl around her shoulders. She was dwarfed by his height and broad shoulders. He gazed down at her. Warmth filled her cheeks.

"I'd like to see you again if you'd be accepting. It's our busy time of year around here. We don't have much free time for..." He glanced away. Scarlett wondered if he had been about to say *courting*. "We men help each other bring our crops in, along with calving, branding, and whatever else needs done. Once the harvesting starts this year, the women plan to meet at whichever farm has the most work and prepare food and help however they can. I believe the Campbell farm is first. I'm sure you'll want to come, too. It'll give you a chance to get to know the other women."

"I'll enjoy that."

"After, if you like, I could drive you home."

After witnessing her coughing spell, Scarlett was surprised he wanted to spend time with her. "I would like that. If it doesn't put you out."

"Not at all." He looked endearingly relieved and bashful at the same time. He glanced at his boots, the street, his horse, as if gathering his nerve to say more. Then he tipped his hat, wished her good night, and stepped off the porch into the night.

Scarlett listened to the sound of his horse's hooves long after it disappeared into the darkness. The wind picked up again, swirling a cloud of dirt around the tail of her skirt. She covered the lower half of her face with her arm and headed to the brides' house. She couldn't stop wondering what her life would look like from this moment on. Without Marianne. Without the factory. Without her health.

Plenty of women never recovered from the factories. Would Travis be interested in a wife too frail for life in Cowboy Creek? Would any man? Did she want to marry if she couldn't be the wife her husband deserved?

Chapter Four

Scarlett sat bolt upright in bed, her heart racing. The nightmare niggled at the edges of her wakefulness. Movement in the darkness. A man's hot breath sliding over her exposed skin. Her wrist chafed from the rope used to bind her to her kidnapper. Every attempt to get away, to lengthen the distance between them, brought pain and fresh terror.

Variations of the same dream tormented her sleep since the day she'd been kidnapped. She dreaded nighttime, knowing the darkness would bring Hoyer's face back to her mind. His leering, pinprick eyes. His grasping hands. His smooth voice disguising a black heart and evil intentions.

She reached for Marianne in the darkness. Before her hands caught hold of the empty blankets, she remembered Marianne wasn't here. It had been three days since she rode away with Nathan to her new home and new life. Three nights with no one to comfort Scarlett when the nightmares wrenched her awake.

She smoothed the blankets out and focused on slowing her ragged breaths. If not for the nightmares, she could get used to sleeping alone without Marianne kicking and hogging the blankets. She had already gotten used to the peaceful solitude of Cowboy Creek. She looked forward to afternoons with Marla, talking and laughing and absorbing the woman's simple wisdom.

Yesterday they butchered and cooked two chickens. Scarlett preferred buying her meat from the grocer where the chickens were already headless and featherless and ready for the stewpot. That wasn't how chicken ended up on the table in Cowboy Creek, so she might as well get used to it. Despite her disgust of the chore, Marla's wry observations kept her laughing the whole time.

The sound that had awakened her—the sound she attributed to the dream—came again. A thump against the wall in the next room followed by a scraping noise.

Scarlett stuffed her arms into the sleeves of her dressing gown. Scuffling came again. Whatever it was wasn't moving around. In the city, she would attribute the noise to a prowler, and she would fill her revolver with bullets before she went to investigate. She couldn't imagine a prowler in Cowboy Creek. Then again, she hadn't expected to be kidnapped either.

Just in case, she took the revolver from the little table by the bed and made sure it was loaded. Most likely an animal had gotten through a hole or loose floorboard, which wouldn't require a gun. She'd chase out the rabbit or possum or skunk, then when it got light, she'd fix the hole.

Oh, she hoped whatever had gotten inside wasn't a skunk. She yanked the blanket off the bed and held it in one hand with the gun in the other. The scuffling came again followed by another thump and more scratching. Yesterday's rain had stopped, but the persistent wind that whistled through the valley all week pulled at the eaves over her head and rattled her already taut nerves.

The first thing she saw when she entered the main room was a looming shape that filled the room. Too big for a skunk or raccoon. Scarlett shrieked, dropped the blanket, and raised the gun. Cool air stirred the hair at the base of her neck.

She exhaled in relief and lowered the gun as she recognized the shape. "Good grief, Scarlett, you nervous nellie," she chided aloud. "You almost shot a tree."

Her relief was short-lived. She had a much bigger problem on her hands than facing down a bear or chasing a skunk outside. She lit the kerosene lantern and surveyed the damage. Spindly branches reached through the broken window into the house. She reached over the broken glass and wood splinters for the broom. She couldn't do much to repair the mess in the darkness. It would take an axe and a saw to get the tree back outside where it belonged. Then there was the matter of fixing the broken window. At least the rain had stopped, and the night air was mild.

The gray light of dawn illuminated the interior of the little house by the time Scarlett secured the window as best she could and laid back down.

Her mind raced from cleaning up the tree to Marianne to Travis to her kidnapper to Dr. Gaetz to Preach and Marla and everyone else she had met since coming west. So much had happened in just a few weeks. She thought of Travis's question about what she wanted. She hadn't given him much of an answer. Even now, she wasn't sure. She came because Marianne told her to.

What now? She couldn't keep making every decision to please her strong-willed sister.

What did she want?

Love. A family. To find a reason to laugh like Marla amid unpleasant chores like skinning chickens or removing a tree from her parlor.

What did she want? It wasn't a hard question. She finally had her answer. She burrowed deeper into the blankets and fell asleep.

After breakfast she helped Marla with the dishes and filled the kindling box. The older woman gave her several sidelong looks, aware something was on her mind. She didn't ask what. She probably assumed Scarlett was missing Marianne—which she always was—and wondering if she would find her own husband among the remaining bachelors.

Instead, Scarlett was estimating how many boards she'd need to cover the broken window. A pane of glass was the best option, but she had no idea where to find one or how she'd pay for it once she did. The situation was God's reminder that she needed to stand on her own two feet. She no longer had Marianne to take charge of a situation. She was twenty-three years old. It was time she took care of her own problems without looking for someone else to swoop in and fix things.

She'd need Preach's help later to order a new pane of glass or repair a busted eave. For now, she'd assess the damage and see how much she could fix herself.

Armed with a handsaw and a hatchet she found in the barn, Scarlett circled the little house. Her heart sank at the sight of the damage. The situation was a lot worse than a broken limb. The huge old tree had split nearly in two with the smaller half leaning precariously over the brides' house. The split had obviously not happened last night. With each storm and high wind, the damage got worse until the smaller half couldn't stand any longer. Another windstorm or heavy snow could bring the entire tree down, taking out the brides' house and part of the barn next door. The tree had to come out, and sooner rather than later.

She almost laughed at the futility of the situation. She was feeling stronger than yesterday, but a handsaw and hatchet wouldn't do much in her hands.

She sighed and climbed onto a broken piece of the tree trunk. At least she could take care of the limbs poking through the window. She shimmied into the split of the tree. It shifted and creaked in protest. She gripped the side of the house with her free hand and second guessed her decision. If the limb broke, she'd only fall a few feet. What bothered her was the possibility of the limbs—some as big around as she was—sliding together and crushing her between them.

She bounced a few times. The huge tree didn't seem to notice. Warily eying the branches over her head, she crept a few feet up the split trunk. Besides a little creaking and shifting, everything remained solid. Emboldened, she crept a little higher until she could put the hatchet on the roof. With the handsaw, she sawed through the smaller limbs she hadn't been able to break off from inside the house. She got used to the shifting of the limbs under her feet. The tree had been standing for decades. She doubted her hundred or so pounds and the little handsaw were enough to bring it down.

She moved farther up the tree, sawing and breaking small limbs as she climbed. When she reached the roofline, she took the hatchet and attacked a few of the larger limbs that scraped the roof tin. She didn't want them doing further damage to the roof until the men could properly remove the tree.

She had to stop often to catch her breath and rest her arms. She didn't want to bring on another coughing spell. She wished she had thought of bringing water with her. Her thirst would have to wait. She wasn't going to stop working to climb down the dangerous tree to get any.

The split in the tree creaked dangerously. A vibration shot up through her legs. She looked through the space between the tree and the roof. Her head spun. She was higher off the ground than she realized. The vibration came again, stronger. The branch she stood on dropped a few inches. Scarlett shrieked and leaped onto the roof. A deafening crack split the air. She raised her arms in front of her as chunks of bark and pulp rained down on her and the roof. With eerie slowness, the crack expanded and grew until the limb on which she'd been standing fell at a sharp angle to the ground.

She ducked and turned away as a myriad of smaller branches rushed past her face and clawed at her hair. The roof vibrated under her feet as the massive tree landed with a thud.

Slowly, Scarlett straightened amidst a forest of broken limbs, pulp, and branches littering the roof. The saw and hatchet were still clenched in her frozen hands. She crept to the edge and peered over. The broken half was now six feet below her. The standing half of the tree was completely out of reach. She was stuck!

Preach had left the house after breakfast. Marla was inside their living quarters behind the trading post. Even if Scarlett had the lung capacity to yell loud enough for Marla to hear, she didn't want to. Marianne had rescued her from a kidnapper. Surely she could figure out a way to get off a roof without calling for help.

She walked the perimeter of the roof, mindful of weak spots, but didn't see a way down besides jumping. It was too far for that. If only she'd used a ladder to climb onto the roof instead of the broken tree. Too late for scolding herself about what she hadn't done.

While she waited for inspiration or for Preach to come back, whichever happened first, she hacked at the broken branches and threw them over the side. Her arms ached and her chest heaved by the time she cleared the smaller branches off the roof. If she were braver, she would jump into the pile she'd made. She'd probably land wrong and break or wrench something and be in a worse fix than she was already.

She eyed the gathering clouds as she worked and prayed it didn't rain. Where was Preach? Or the Whitamore children? What about Marla? Wasn't it about time for a trip to the privy?

She was about ready to swallow her pride and let out a shout when she heard a horse. Thank goodness. Preach was back. From her vantage point she could see quite a distance through the thinning leaves of the trees lining the narrow, jagged street. It didn't take long for her rescuer to ride into view. It wasn't Preach. Her heart skipped a beat at the sight of Travis. She walked gingerly to the front of the house and waited until his horse was directly below her. "Yoo hoo," she called.

Travis jerked the horse to a stop. Scarlett's face warmed, startled all over again by how handsome he was. If a woman was interested in a husband, she'd be hard pressed to find a better looking one. She wiggled her fingers at him.

He took off his hat and tilted his head to look at her.

"Nice day for a ride," she said lightly.

He smiled. "Nice day for roof sitting."

"That's what I thought."

He rested his large, calloused hands on the saddle pommel. "What are you doing up there?"

She pointed at the standing half of the tree behind her. "Part of this tree decided to fall through the window last night."

He grimaced. "Where's the ladder?"

She lifted her shoulders. "In the barn, I expect. I didn't think I'd need it. Until the limb I climbed up on broke and fell out of reach."

He shook his head in wonder at the tree. "I reckon we need to make time to take that hazard out of there before it causes a lot more trouble than a broken window."

"In the meantime maybe we could get me off this roof."

He replaced his hat and grinned. "That does seem like the first order of business. I could fetch the ladder. Or I could come a little closer and you could jump into my arms."

Scarlett pressed her lips together. Why'd he have to be so stinking adorable? "Get the ladder."

He tipped his hat. "Yes, ma'am." He dismounted and sauntered to the barn, whistling as he went. Scarlett attributed the flutter in her stomach to the thought of rescue and not how much she enjoyed watching him walk away. It didn't help that he seemed to know the effect his walking away had on her.

Within a minute or two he reappeared with a long ladder. He propped it against the side of the house. Scarlett reached for the top rung. Travis held up a hand to stop her. "Oh, no, you don't. I'm coming after you."

"Oh, no, you won't." She couldn't imagine how his helping would be any better than climbing down herself. "I'm perfectly capable—"

He was already on his way up. "I'll never hear the end of it from Marla or your sister if you fall with me standing right here."

He reached the top of the ladder and held out his hand. With a sigh of defeat, Scarlett turned her back to him and perched on his shoulder. Though she couldn't see his face, she knew he was grinning all the way down. She protested weakly, though she enjoyed the situation nearly as much. When he reached the bottom, he put his hands on her waist and set her on the ground. He kept his hands in place a little longer than he needed to. Scarlett didn't mind.

He plucked a leaf from her hair. "That wasn't so bad, was it?"

Scarlett smoothed her hair away from her face. "I'm just happy to be back on the ground."

"And I'm happy I was the cowpoke who happened by at the right time to get you there."

She was happy, too, that he was the one. If only he wouldn't look at her like he knew how much she enjoyed his teasing. She was shaking harder on the ground next to him than she had when the tree fell out from under her. He probably knew that too.

Travis grabbed the door handle. "Show me where that tree came through the window and I'll fix it."

"Oh, no, I intend to—"

He was already going inside. "I have the tools and lumber at home. Won't be no time I can have a new one set for you."

She followed him into the little house. "I'm sure you do, but I—"

He turned and faced her, silencing the words on her lips. "You don't like asking for help, do you?"

She squared her shoulders. "As a matter of fact, I do not. Marianne has taken care of both of us my whole life. It's time I learn to do things for myself."

"Sounds like a great plan. In the meantime, I'll build a new window frame and install it tomorrow. Then after harvest is over and we have the time, I'll take you out to my place and teach you how to build the next window frame yourself. Now, where's your hammer? I'll close up this window to keep you dry for tonight."

"Oh, dear. I left Preach's hatchet and saw on the roof."

He rolled his eyes and chuckled. "You stay here. I'll be right back."

Later, if she didn't forget, Scarlett would get annoyed by the teasing. For now, she'd enjoy watching him walk away again.

Chapter Five

Scarlett put her hands on either side of her face to see through the glass into the darkened storefront. As far as she could tell, the only occupied buildings in Cowboy Creek were the trading post, the meetinghouse, and the brides' house. This morning after delivering the milk to Marla and Preach from the two cows in their barn she noticed the tiny building across the street. Unlike the rest of the dwellings arranged haphazardly along the narrow street, this one didn't look abandoned or about to fall in.

Yesterday, Travis brought the new window and installed it on the back wall of the brides' house. Every time Scarlett looked through it, she thought of his large, capable hands wrapped around the hammer.

As he worked, he told stories about the characters around the small town where he grew up. He'd had a hard life, but he seemed to take everything he'd been through in stride. She wondered, though. A person's journey affected who they became. How had his journey to this point in his life shaped him, and would she ever know the whole story?

Just as he finished the window, Preach and three other men arrived to fell the remainder of the tree behind the house. They left it where it landed facing the creek. Everyone was too busy to do more than that for the time being. It needed to season anyway to make good firewood.

Scarlett dragged the limbs of the tree to a burn pile far from the house and barn. She'd done everything she could think of to occupy her time. She didn't have fabric for sewing, and with only herself to look after, it didn't take long to complete her daily chores. She helped Marla as needed, but Marla joked repeatedly that with all the brides coming and going, she was caught up on her chores through the end of the year.

Scarlett sidled along the dirt path in front of the building to get a better view inside through the wavy old glass.

"Do you want to borrow a book?"

She dropped her hands, startled. Candace Whitamore, the twelve-year-old daughter of the mill owner and his wife, approached from the direction of the creek that flowed past the town.

Scarlett stepped away from the building and waited for the girl to reach her. "Borrow a book? Do you mean like a library?"

Candace nodded and smiled proudly. "Can you imagine? A little spot like Cowboy Creek with a real library."

"A lot of cities don't have lending libraries. How did Cowboy Creek manage it?"

"I suppose it isn't a real library. Mrs. DeSantis arrived from Cincinnati with trunks and trunks of books. She didn't have anywhere to store them at her cabin, so she and her husband decided to store them here where they'd be available to everybody."

Scarlett moved back to the window to peer inside. "Amazing."

"The door's unlocked," Candace said. "We can go in if you like."

Scarlett chuckled to herself. Too many years in the city made her forget communities like Cowboy Creek didn't have locked doors. She followed Candace inside. She'd never been in a library, even a pseudo-library in the Rocky Mountain foothills with only a private collection of books available for patrons. She stopped in the doorway in surprise. The small space was crammed full of furniture, looking wildly out of place in the crooked, rough-sided building.

A polished, intricately carved bookcase overflowed with books. Every flat surface in the room held stacks of more books. As her eyes adjusted to the gloom, she saw two small tables in the middle of the room. One had a chair pushed against it. The other had two. On the smaller table was a ledger, a closed pot of ink, and a pen.

Candace placed a proprietary hand on the ledger. Her slender face was at the awkward stage between child and young woman, but Scarlett could see she would be quite pretty when she grew up, if not beautiful. Especially with the smile she now wore. "This is where people write the title of the book they're taking and the date. If anyone else wants to borrow that book, they'll know who has it and when to expect it back.

"Mrs. DeSantis comes once or twice a week to straighten up and make sure the mice and possums haven't overrun the building. She's very particular about her books. Last month she found a spider's nest in a book of maps of the Orient. She was very exasperated with that spider."

Scarlett ran a finger along the spines of a shelf of books. "Amazing," she repeated. "I can't believe one person owns so many books."

"None of us can. I helped Mrs. DeSantis set everything up." The girl's chin lifted importantly. "I keep an eye on things when she can't come. It's harvest time. No one has been here in weeks." Pulled

She pulled out a book near Scarlett's hand and opened the heavy volume. "Would you like to borrow something? You can keep it as long as you like."

Scarlett looked at the tiny type in the book. Even though she was looking at it upside down, she doubted she would be able to understand the meaning of the words. She and Marianne had only attended a few years of grammar school, and even then, they missed more days than not. She couldn't admit such a thing to a child. When no one was around, she'd choose an easier one to take back to the brides' house and practice her reading.

"I don't know if I'll have much time to read."

Candace closed the book and put it back on the shelf. "Me either. Mama keeps us busy. Papa says once harvest is over there'll be time for relaxing. He said at the end of harvest, the whole community goes to Ruby City to sell the surplus. Even us, though we don't raise anything. He said we'll have grain and feed to barter and sell. We'll stay overnight in a hotel and eat in restaurants and shop in real stores." Her sapphire blue eyes danced with excitement. "I can't wait. You'll go with us, of course."

Scarlett wasn't sure about that. She wouldn't have anything to sell or barter, and she didn't have money for a night in a hotel. She couldn't insert herself into Marianne's trip with Nathan, though Marianne would insist she was welcome. An image of Travis's handsome face flitted across her mind. Naturally, he'd be going. He had already proven he was interested in her. Would he make his intentions known by then? What would she say if he did?

She liked Travis more with each interaction. She was definitely attracted to him. Even if that were enough of a foundation on which to base a marriage, he deserved more of a wife than she'd ever be. With her physical limitations, it was better to accept now she could never marry before her heart got involved.

She pushed the discouraging thoughts aside and let Candace's excitement rub off on her. She could only imagine how much the girl was looking forward to a trip to Ruby City after living in this remote place for months. She was probably bursting at the chance to see new sights and new faces, especially boys' faces.

Candace went to a low bureau, its surface piled high with thinner books with brightly colored covers. "These are the books I like to read. They're actual stories about men and women finding adventure. Not history books or maps or poetry I can't understand. They're not just for children. You might find something you like for after the harvest when we have time to read."

Scarlett hoped Candace hadn't deduced she wasn't a good reader. She opened a few books at random. "I like adventure stories too. And romance." She arched her eyebrows and grinned. "It gets lonesome in the little house without Marianne. Back home, she and I got up early every morning, went straight to work, worked all day, then came home and went to bed. We didn't have time for our own adventures."

Candace sighed, her eyes on the book spines. "The same for me. My days used to be filled with school and chores and friends. Now it's just chores. I'm thankful for these books and for Mrs. DeSantis."

It must be so difficult it was to grow up here with no other children. No school. Especially for Candace. She was at the age where she was thinking about boys and her future. She must've realized unless other families moved to the area, she had no hope of finding a husband in the middle of nowhere.

"It must've been hard to leave your friends behind."

Candace turned a book around to read the title. "It was at first. Much of the reason we're here is because of me."

"You?"

"I got into trouble back home. Some of my friends weren't very nice. We caused mischief at school and around the neighborhood. Mama was worried I'd get into real trouble she couldn't get me out of if she didn't do something."

"I can't imagine you being like that."

"That's what Mama thought. She'd say, 'Candace Caroline, I raised you better than that. Whatever happened to my darling little girl?' I always wanted to say, 'I ate her'."

Scarlett gasped, then she and the girl laughed.

"I never said it," Candace explained quickly. "Mama would've washed my mouth out with soap. She doesn't tolerate belligerence."

Scarlett laughed again. "She sounds like a good mama."

Candace sighed. "She is. I'm glad now that we came here. I was so mad in the beginning I wouldn't speak to her or anybody except Marla—I mean, Mrs. Dodds. She was so nice to me. She taught me how to cook and bake. Mostly she taught me to value myself and respect others. She never said as much, but she showed me I'm worth more than stealing candy from the corner store and pushing little kids around. Mama wasn't the only one who didn't like the girl I had turned into. I'm glad the old Candace is back."

"That's very mature for a girl your age."

Candace shrugged. "It's exhausting being mad all the time. It takes a lot less work to smile and be kind to the people who love you."

Scarlett clasped her hands. "I think I'm going to like getting to know you, Candace."

Candace blushed. "May I ask you a question, Miss Sanders?"

Scarlett's stomach tightened, not sure what to expect. She doubted she had the same sage advice to offer as Marla. "Certainly."

"Mama would say it's none of my business and children don't have the right to ask grown folks certain things…"

"It's all right," Scarlett assured her as her words tapered off. "You can ask me whatever you want."

"It's just that—I don't understand why women keep coming. I understand why the men want women to come.

There are none around and they need wives to help with the work. But why do the women come? There are men in the city. Why come all this way when you can find a man anywhere?"

Scarlett laughed.

Candace's eyes widened. "I didn't mean any disrespect."

"No, dear, you didn't offend me. It's a logical question. First off, I don't think the men want women just to help with the work, though I'm sure that's a consideration. Most of them want companionship. Someone to build a life with and support them in every endeavor. You've probably been lonely for your friends and schoolmates since you came here."

The girl nodded solemnly.

"I don't know about the others," Scarlett continued, "but Marianne and I came because Marianne was worried about me. Working in the laundry had made me sick. Marianne didn't like her job either. She wanted us to have options. I expect that's a big reason for why the other women come. In the city, a woman pretty much has to live the life she was born to. Out here there's a chance for something new. A whole new life."

"But it's still more work. That seems to be all life is for women. Work. And babies." Her lip curled in distaste.

Scarlett nearly laughed, but she saw how serious the matter was for Candace. "Yes, but it's work we choose to do, not work we're forced to do."

"And you want to get married."

Scarlett sighed, unsure of how honest she should be with a child. The girl probably couldn't understand a woman choosing not to marry. "Since I've grown up, I haven't had time to think about beaus or marriage. I always figured if I was meant to marry the Lord would make it happen."

Now, it didn't look like it would.

Candace tilted her head. "Marla says we can't sit around and expect the Lord to do everything for us. He expects us to put in the work if we want something."

Scarlett laughed. "I'm going to like getting to know Marla better."

Candace beamed. "Oh, you will. She's wonderful. I wish she was my granny."

Scarlett smoothed her hand over the girl's pale blond hair. "She probably thinks of you as her granddaughter."

The sound of an approaching wagon drew their attention. They moved to the open door. "It's Mr. and Mrs. Jamison," Candace said. "They have a hog farm down the road, which you can smell easy enough when the wind's blowing the wrong way. They go to Good Hope almost every week to sell hams and sausages. Sometimes they invite J.T. and me to ride along. Not Annie. Mama says she's too little." She went outside as she talked with Scarlett behind her.

Sawyer Jamison pulled the wagon to a stop in front of the trading post and jumped out.

Candace called out to Katie, Sawyer's beautiful, petite wife. She waved at them. "Good afternoon, Candace. Oh, Scarlett, you're the person I wanted to see."

Sawyer lifted his hand to assist Kate out of the wagon and then went inside the trading post. Katie, Candace, and Scarlett met in the middle of the street. "At the general store Mrs. Boebert told me Doc Gaetz will be in town tomorrow. She thought you might want to come in and visit with him."

Scarlett bristled at the idea that her health problems were common knowledge in the area, yet keeping any type of secret would be nearly impossible around here. Despite her annoyance, she was thankful for the chance to see the doctor. "I'm sure he'll want to check my progress."

She didn't add that she was eager for him to do so as well.

"Mrs. Boebert said he'll see patients at the hotel. You won't have any trouble finding him. Sheriff Tatum wants women to avoid driving through the countryside unescorted. The gang that kidnapped you and Marianne is locked up, but he's leery of women traveling alone until he's satisfied no rogue members are out there."

"I'll ask Marla and Preach to take me."

"No need. Sawyer and I took the liberty of stopping at Travis's place on our way by. He said he's free and he'll be happy to take you. He'll pick you up first thing tomorrow morning. Well, I must go. I have business with Marla." She hurried away before Scarlett could protest. "We'll be praying for a good report from the doctor," she said over her shoulder. "Nice seeing you, Candace."

Chapter Six

D r. Gaetz moved the stethoscope over Scarlett's back. She breathed deeply as instructed and tried to still the wild beating of her heart. The white-haired man had barely looked her in the eye during his examination and he hadn't seemed pleased with her answers to his questions. She missed Marianne's comforting presence, but Marianne wasn't here. She didn't even know Scarlett was. Scarlett planned to keep it that way. Marianne had more important things to focus on now without holding Scarlett's hand through every stressful situation.

Finally, the doctor looped the stethoscope around his neck and circled the table to face her. "Miss Sanders, I'm afraid I have nothing conclusive to tell you. Your lung capacity is very limited for a woman your age. You look healthy enough, and maybe you are."

He took a deep breath. Scarlett clasped her hands within the folds of her skirt. Despite her bravado that this was her problem and she would handle it on her own, she wasn't sure she was ready to hear a grave prognosis alone. Travis was outside. He had parked the carriage in the shade and told her he'd be waiting when she finished. How could she sit in stoic silence next to him all the way home if Dr. Gaetz gave her the worst news possible?

"There's no way of knowing the extent of the damage done to your lungs working in that factory for as long as you did. During my training, I treated many young women just like you. Some had no lasting effects while others—well, I don't need to tell you many of them didn't enjoy long lives as most young people expect to."

Scarlett pursed her lips around a whimper of fear. She wasn't sure if Dr. Gaetz heard or if he had no time or patience to indulge a hysterical woman. He continued with no sign of sympathy.

"I don't make it a habit of promising long life and vigor to any of my patients. No one calls for me unless they know something's wrong and want it fixed. You told me you exhibited complications before you left Cincinnati." His grim expression softened by a degree. "I don't mean to scare you or cause unnecessary worry. I just want to you to be aware of the limits required by your body that most other women won't experience." He patted her shoulder before turning away to put his stethoscope on the table next to him.

"What can I…Is there anything…"

She didn't know what to ask.

He straightened his tools before looking back at her. "It's a hard life out here, Miss Sanders, even for strong women. You may want to consider moving in with your sister. If that's not possible, you can go back to the city where you'll have other, less strenuous, options for earning a living."

Scarlett didn't interrupt to tell him she would never become a charity case to Marianne and Nathan. How humiliating! And moving back to Cincinnati without Marianne would be just as difficult.

"You could become a nanny or a teacher," the doctor continued. "Or a seamstress in a dress shop. Something that doesn't involve the back breaking work required should you become a farmer's wife here and work yourself into an early grave."

An early grave.

She pressed her lips together to keep them from trembling. She didn't want to die. Not here and not in a dress shop in the city. "I know other girls who recovered completely once they got out of the factories. Is that a possibility for me as well?"

He nodded thoughtfully, though she could see he wasn't overly hopeful. "Of course. Again, there's no way of knowing. Only God can see inside the human body. My tools give me an idea of what's going on, but it's a very dim picture. With rest, fresh air, and exercise, your lungs may completely repair themselves. Our bodies are amazing, resilient machines. But it may be too late. I'm sorry, Miss Sanders. I wish I could look into the future and tell you your lungs will completely recover, and you'll live to see your children's grandchildren. But I can't. My best advice is for you to go back to the city and marry a wealthy man, so you'll never have to lift a finger in manual labor again."

He chuckled, genuinely amused by the comment, and left the room. Scarlett fastened the buttons of her bodice and pulled her shawl over her shoulders. She stood on trembling legs and willed herself not to cry. She walked out of the hotel into the sunshine in a daze.

Wealthy husband, indeed! She hadn't found one during her first twenty-three years in the city. She didn't expect to find one in the next. Nor did she want to.

At the corner of the building Travis leaned against the carriage they had borrowed from Preach and Marla making notations in a small notebook. When he heard her approach he stuffed the notebook and pencil into his pocket and directed that broad enigmatic smile at her.

Scarlett's spirit lifted. During the drive to Good Hope, she had gotten to know him a little better. He was interesting and smart and had made the time go faster with amusing anecdotes and stories of growing up surrounded by what sounded like a diverse group of characters. He seemed just as interested in getting to know her. Scarlett was flattered by his attention, but after Dr. Gaetz's grim prognosis, she couldn't entertain the notion of marriage.

She didn't want to work herself into an early grave and leave a husband and children to get along without her. It wouldn't be fair to any of them. She might not even be strong enough to bear children. She hadn't thought to ask the doctor that question. It wasn't likely he'd have given her an answer anyway. But men expected children, especially the men of Cowboy Creek. Without future generations, in a few years the community would dry up and blow away in the next fierce wind.

She pasted a warm smile on her face, determined not to show her distress over Dr. Gaetz's words. Questions and doubts ricocheted inside her head. She wished she could talk to Marianne. That was out of the question. If Marianne even suspected Scarlett needed her, she would insist Scarlett move in with her and Nathan and they keep her in relative comfort until her frail body gave out. Scarlett would rather die in a factory than let that happen.

She'd keep quiet until she knew for herself if she was improving or not. Dr. Gaetz had admitted everything he said was conjecture. He didn't know more than she did about the damage done to her body. After a few weeks or months of rest and fresh air, she could be as right as rain. Or the damage she suffered could be irreparable. Either way, no amount of worrying and fretting from her sister would make a bit of difference. She wouldn't tell her sister or Travis or anyone else about something that, if proven true, couldn't be changed or undone.

Travis stepped onto the sidewalk to offer Scarlett his elbow. His heart nearly skipped a beat. She sure was pretty. About the prettiest gal he'd ever seen, and he'd seen plenty. Her auburn hair was twisted into a heavy knot at the back of her head. He couldn't tell much about it under her bonnet except that it was a few shades darker than her sister's, and it looked thick with a bit of curl. He'd always been partial to auburn hair with a bit of curl.

Travis wasn't bashful around women either like most of the other men in Cowboy Creek. Obviously the first six women hadn't been intended for him since he and Lonnie Fanshaw were the only bachelors left standing without a woman. After all these months, his wait for a bride could be over if Scarlett Sanders returned his interest like he hoped.

She set her delicate hand on his arm and smiled at him. Travis's heart surged again. She sure looked interested. He knew women pretty well. He knew what they found amusing. What could send them into a rage one minute and a fit of giggles the next.

What he couldn't understand was why they didn't come out and say what was on their minds instead of leaving a man to puzzle over it and never reach the right conclusion. Something was definitely on Scarlett's mind now. Her vivid cornflower blue eyes were brooding and somber and belied the bright smile she directed at him.

His gut tightened. Whatever Doc Gaetz said wasn't what she had wanted to hear. He waited until they were settled in the rig before he spoke, keeping his tone light. "How'd it go? I hope Doc gave you a good report."

Her gaze flitted to a barrel of rakes in front of the hardware store, then to a crooked shutter that had come loose from the side of the building that no one had bothered to nail back into place. "Nothing more than what I already suspected." Her tone was light, too, though the corners of her mouth had gone tight. "My lungs have been damaged from working in factories. Dust, pollen, woodsmoke, chemicals—it all aggravates the problem."

Travis watched closely, listening for what she didn't say. "What can he do about it?"

She lifted her rigid shoulders. "The first time I saw him, he gave me a vile-tasting tonic that was supposed to help clear my lungs. I don't know if it works or not. He didn't have much confidence in it himself. Rest and fresh air are about the only things that make a difference. Most of the girls I worked with improved as soon as they left the factories."

She smiled brightly. Too brightly.

What about the others, Travis wondered.

Scarlett averted her gaze, maybe thinking on those women, the ones who didn't improve. Travis wished he had been in the room when Doc Gaetz talked to her. Her medical condition was none of his business, of course. Not yet. They weren't married. They weren't committed to each other. He stole a glance at her. Her jaw was clenched and her eyes fixed straight ahead. Travis wanted to tell her that even though they didn't know each other that well and she had no reason to trust him, he'd like to commit to her. He'd like to marry her and help her through whatever bad report she might be facing.

After a long moment of staring into the distance, Scarlett took a deep breath and brought her attention back to him. "I feel like I'm getting stronger every day. I haven't had one of my coughing fits for days. With more rest and fresh air, I'll be fine. No need for worry."

She sounded like she was trying to convince herself as much as him. It reminded Travis of the way Mama used to talk when she didn't want him to know how sick she was. Mama had tried to protect him from the cold realities of life, even when he was a wee whippersnapper. She wanted him to believe he was a regular boy like all the others in town. But he wasn't. He wasn't like the boys in school who pointed at him and laughed and pushed him down and called him terrible names he didn't understand.

It didn't take long, though, to figure out what those names meant. It took even less to realize they were right. He *was* different. Tainted by the circumstances of his birth. Unacceptable. Dirty. The day he figured it out, he ran home from school—his shirt soiled with dirt and blood and tears—and told Mama he was never going back to that school. She saw from the look on his young face there was so dissuading him. She never had the fight in her to force him to do what he didn't want to.

When she took sick, she tried to hide the coughs, the weakness, the shallow breathing. She did her best to disguise her weight loss with flowing skirts and heavy makeup and boisterous talk. Mr. Keplinger didn't generally hire doctors to come to the saloon to look at his girls. They weren't worth the money. Nor did he want word getting out that the women who worked upstairs were anything less than healthy and as fresh as the morning dew. The fact that he called the doctor for Mama told Travis the situation was grave, and Mama meant more to Mr. Keplinger than either of them let on.

He hid in the wardrobe that day during the examination. The word *consumption* didn't mean anything in and of itself, but from the doctor's expression and the way the blood drained from Mama's face at the mention of it, Travis knew something terrible was happening. He wouldn't have his beloved mama much longer.

The other women in the saloon saw to more of the customers and did their best to keep Mr. Keplinger and the men downstairs from realizing Mama wasn't pulling her weight. She slept more and ate less. Yet she continued to tell Travis everything was fine. She'd be back to her old self in no time. Just like Scarlett was doing now. Mama told him what she wanted to be true. A little rest, a little time, and a little less of his hovering, and everything would be all right.

Travis sighed inwardly. He wasn't sure he could go through that emotional turmoil again. He didn't know if he could take it. He didn't know if he wanted to.

Chapter Seven

The wagon veered off the main road onto a barely discernible path. Scarlett's fingers reflexively clenched around the strings of her reticule. Her heart raced as images of another man in another carriage flashed across her mind. A man who promised to give her and Marianne a ride to Cowboy Creek only to kidnap them with plans to force them to work in saloons. When Marianne resisted, the kidnapper had shoved her out of the carriage and rode away with Scarlett. Scarlett hadn't known then if she would see her sister or freedom again. If Nathan Lake hadn't come along when he did and found Marianne in the road screaming Scarlett's name, Scarlett may not have been rescued. She wouldn't have been the first woman on the frontier to become a victim of men with evil intentions.

She reminded herself she was perfectly safe with Travis. He wasn't dangerous or a kidnapper. She loosened her fingers from around her purse strings. She wondered if her heart would leap into her throat for the rest of her life any time a man reached past her to take a saltshaker from the table.

"I hope you don't mind, but I thought we'd take a little detour past my place," he said without a hint of malice in his easy smile. A rakish smile that was rapidly growing on her. How could she have thought for a minute she had anything to fear? "It's not far. This way'll get us there quicker than staying on the main road. We'll see more of the countryside, too."

She smiled at the hope in his cinnamon-colored eyes. "That'd be nice." She set her hand on her head to keep her hat in place as the ruts in the road became more pronounced.

As the elevation rose, the valley spread out in front of them. Splashes of yellow peppered the rolling hillside. Soon oranges and reds and purple would color the trees as the nights grew cooler and the hint of the approaching winter grew stronger.

"This is lovely," Scarlett enthused. "So different from what I'm used to. I can see for miles."

"See that ribbon of water?" He pointed through a stand of trees. "That's my stream that comes off the one that flows from Cowboy Creek. I reckon it's not my stream. I didn't have anything to do with putting it there. In a few weeks when the leaves are gone, you can see the route it takes all the way to the backside of my meadow. We got enough rain this summer that it never stopped flowing. Every previous summer I've been here, the creek dried up to barely a trickle. There are several wide places that hold water, though, no matter how dry the season. My stock has never gone without water and the well in the yard has never gone dry."

Scarlett kept her eyes on the landscape as she listened. Water meant provision and prosperity. Without saying as much out loud, he was letting her know he could provide for a wife.

The trail became increasingly bumpy travel. Once Scarlett nearly lurched out of the seat. "One of these days, I'll have to fill that hole," Travis quipped with a guilty smile.

Before she could answer, they rounded a copse of trees, and the valley came into full view. A small cabin and outbuildings were laid out in a regimental grid as if in consideration of convenience and safety from marauders and predators.

"Oh my, Travis. It's beautiful. Did you do it all yourself?"

Pride swelled his chest. "Not all. We men help each other as best we can."

"It must take a hard man to build a life out of nothing."

"I reckon you're right." The look he gave her was thoughtful and intense.

Scarlett looked away. She shouldn't have let him bring her here. He was getting the wrong idea. It was written all over his face. It was probably written all over hers as well. She liked Travis. She liked him more today than after the day he helped her off the roof. But he needed someone else. It didn't only take a hard man to build a life here. It took a strong woman. A woman like Eliza Waring. Or formidable Marianne who battled a gang of kidnappers to save her sister. Scarlett wasn't strong enough to save a kitten from a tree. She needed to tell Travis right now she appreciated the tour and the ride to Good Hope, but if he was looking for a wife, he needed to keep looking.

Dr. Gaetz was right. Her constitution was only tough enough for teaching school or working as a nanny or clerking in a shop somewhere. She wasn't built for the frontier.

She looked at him and her heart melted a little. Her resolve faded. He was so handsome. And ambitious and determined. If he was thinking what it looked like he was thinking, she could be throwing away her one chance at happiness by settling on a safe life in the city. Was it a mistake she would forever regret?

Before she could get the thoughts straight in her head, he set the brake and jumped down from the borrowed buggy. He circled the backend to her side and reached for her hand. When her feet touched the ground, he held onto her a few moments before letting go. Scarlett's heart surged at the strength in his fingers, the breadth of his shoulders. She could stand and look at him all day. Oh, what was she thinking? She needn't make this decision any harder than it had to be.

He led her across the yard to a pump near the cabin door. He primed the pump, then filled the cup hanging on the hook and handed it to her. "There's a pump in the house, too, but I like using this one this time of year."

Scarlett looked around the yard over the top of the tin cup as he pumped fresh water into the trough for the horse. Her gaze drifted back to his rugged form as he worked the pump handle. His arms and back rippled with corded muscles. Travis glanced over his shoulder at her. Warmth flooded her cheeks. She looked hastily away, but not before that dashing smile lit up his features. A man like Travis had to be used to attention from women. She was sending the wrong message by letting that attention come from her.

He stopped working the pump and unhitched the horse from the carriage. While he led the horse to the trough, Scarlett used the time to compose herself.

"Shall we?" He offered his elbow. His eyes gleamed with pleased humor. Scarlett slipped her hand around his arm and kept her eyes averted as he led her to the house.

At the front door, her stoicism slipped. She let go of Travis's arm and ran her hand over the smooth wood of the door. "Oh, my! This is exquisite. I've never seen anything like it." The door was built from three wide, hand-grooved planks that fit each other and the door lintel as snugly as any fancy house she'd seen in the city. It was sanded smooth as glass and varnished with a glossy lacquer that shone in the afternoon sun.

Travis ran his thumb down a groove to clean away a cobweb. "I'm mighty happy with the way this door turned out. I ordered the lacquer from the hardware store in Good Hope. Took four months to get it. Over the next few years, the door will continue to darken until it's nearly black." He pushed open the door and stepped back for her to enter the cabin ahead of him. "I came across a felled walnut tree the summer I first found this place. Didn't know what I'd do with it at first. You never can tell what a tree will be good for until you split it open. Could'a been rotten for all I knew. I hauled it over to Lonnie's and had him split it for me. As soon as I saw the grain, I knew I had a work of art. Spent that whole first winter on it."

"It's definitely a work of art. Something to be proud of."

"Thank you. I am proud of it. I do woodworking during the winter months when I'm snowbound and can't do much else. I set up a couple sawhorses right here in the house and work on projects as time allows. The door was first, but I've done a few things since then."

Scarlett gazed around the smooth paneled walls and dark polished floors. A few rugs and the cabin would be quite homey. Her gaze came to rest on the table. Without waiting for an invitation, she stepped across the room to the area set up for cooking and eating. "Like this table? Did you do it as well?"

"I didn't have much growing up. Mama and I always lived—well, we never had a home of our own. Once I did, I wanted to create unique pieces that made the place completely mine."

Scarlett's fingers trailed across the smooth tabletop. The wood pieces had been angled so they fit together in a starburst pattern. Each board was marked with knots and swirls that were unique but complemented the others. She never dreamed she'd see such a creation in a cabin on the frontier.

Travis didn't try to hide his pleasure at her admiration. She was glad about that. She didn't appreciate false pride. He wouldn't have put as much time and effort into the tabletop if it wasn't a labor of love. No point in pretending otherwise.

"This table took up my second winter," he told her. "It's oak. Heavy as a half-grown calf. Like the door, it will be here long after I'm gone." He ran a forefinger around the edge. "The pattern reminds me of a wagon wheel. I thought it was fitting since I've come so far from where I started."

"Well, I love it. I'm in awe of the artistry."

"Didn't expect as much from a cowpoke?"

She nearly denied it until she saw the humor in his eyes. She smiled back. "I guess I didn't."

"I suppose there are more productive ways for a man to spend his time than dedicating a whole winter to a couple pieces of furniture when something simpler and more functional will do."

"I disagree. I mean, if a person has the skills and the material, I don't see why he shouldn't build something that gives him satisfaction and pleasure."

"I'd much rather be doing this than tramping through the woods hunting and trapping all winter."

Her mind filled with an image of him working on a project—a cradle, perhaps—while snow piled up outside and a baby blanket spilled from her knitting needles. She hastily pushed the image aside. Marriage and babies weren't for her.

"Where did you learn this kind of craftsmanship?" she asked to clear her head. "Your pa—"

"No," he nearly snapped. He smiled to soften the brusque reply. "I, uh, knew a man in town. He was a—regular customer where—uh, where my mama worked."

He stoked the fire in the stove to life, then slid a kettle onto the hot plate. Scarlett got the impression he wanted to get her eyes off him for a few moments, which was odd since until now he had seemed to like the attention she gave him.

"He had a little business in town," Travis said after Scarlett took a seat at the table. "Made all manner of furniture. Cabinets, tables, chairs, chests. Anything out of wood, he could build it. He was known for his grandfather clocks. Folks would come from all over to get their hands on one. Heirlooms, they were called. Some customers would wait up to a year for him to fill an order. You could say he took me under his wing, especially after Mama got bad off. Taught me a lot. Seemed I had a natural knack for it. I sure do love it."

He took two tip cups off the shelf. "Sorry I don't have any pie or cookies or even biscuits and jam to offer you with the coffee. I didn't think about entertaining a lady at my table today. I don't have much time for baking. I'm no good at it anyway."

"Coffee is fine."

"I should've bought something at the bakery or the café before we left town."

For such a self-assured man, he sure seemed nervous. Was it her? Maybe he wasn't as confident around women as he portrayed. "Really, Travis, it's all right."

He sat down on the other side of the table. Scarlett ran her hand across the smooth surface of the table. She could barely feel the seams. "You definitely have a knack for woodworking. Or you were a good student. I imagine you would have people coming from all around, too, if they saw the things you built."

His cinnamon-colored eyes warmed. "I wouldn't mind doing something like that. Setting up my own shop. There's a fella in Good Hope, Tyrus Hanks. He builds furniture for folks around here. Does good work, but he doesn't have much imagination. Mostly builds what he can put together fast to sell to folks who don't have other options. I understand the need, but I'd prefer to build quality furniture. One-of-a-kind pieces like the fellow I was telling you about. I just don't have time to work on pieces for anyone but myself while running this place."

"More's the pity. Once your farm's built up, you should have more time to create beautiful pieces."

Travis's gaze intensified as he studied her. Scarlett's heart stilled. She could almost see the gears turning in his head. Building up his farm was exactly why he'd sent for a bride. It was why she was sitting here.

"Where did you grow up?" she blurted. Anything to get his mind off the path it seemed to have taken.

He stood and went to the stove to pour the coffee. "Lawrence, Kansas. A little frontier town you probably never heard of." He set a pitcher of cream and sugar bowl in front of her. "I never knew my pa. He died before I was born. Mama didn't talk about him much except to say I was the spitting image of him. I wouldn't know. Never saw a picture."

"It must be hard for a boy to grow up without a pa."

He stared into his coffee cup for a long moment. Scarlett inwardly kicked herself for bringing up a potentially sore subject. The loss was apparently still raw, even after all these years. "Could've been worse I reckon," he finally answered. "Everyone around town knew Mama and me. Several of the locals watched out for me. Gave me advice. Taught me things boys need to know."

Scarlett stayed quiet as Travis took a careful sip of the boiling coffee. She knew he wasn't through. It looked like he was measuring how much to tell her.

He looked up and gave her a smile though not as easily as before. "I had it better than most in my situation. After Mama got sick, Mr. Keplinger let me stay on and work for him and some of the other men around town, including the furniture builder I told you about. Some of them didn't treat me so well. They'd give me work, then claim they didn't like the way I did things so they could get out of paying me. That's how things go when you don't have anybody to stand up for you. People take advantage. If I ever have young'uns, I'll do my level best to be there for them and not leave them at the mercy of those who want to use them."

"What did you mean when you said you built the tabletop in the shape of a wheel to remind you of how far you'd come? Do you mean how far you traveled from Kansas? Or—how different your life is now from how it started?"

He watched her for a moment, measuring his words. "Nothing out here is like where I came from. The land. The work. The people. Folks treated me well enough, considering, but the faces were always changing. If I made friends or got used to someone, they could be gone by the time I woke up the next morning. Cowboy Creek isn't like that. Like this cabin." He looked around the four walls before bringing his gaze back to her. "One man can only do so much. But nine. Nine of us can build an empire. That's what we aim to do. Our reasons for ending up here are different, but in ways I suppose they're the same. We couldn't find a place to fit in the cities and towns where we came from. Like you women, I expect.

"The night Rase brought up the idea of sending for brides, I went home wondering what kind of woman would answer an ad to marry a man she never met. I thought the women who came would be a bunch of castoffs. Broken. Desperate. Women nobody wanted. I never thought they'd have the same reasons as us men for coming here."

Scarlett blew the steam off her coffee cup and sipped carefully. She thought of Candace asking her yesterday why the women came. She wasn't a castoff or desperate, but she supposed she was a little broken. The other women came west of their own volition. Scarlett came because Marianne told her to. The way she'd made every decision in her life. Marianne was the courageous one. The one who figured out what she wanted, then went after it. Scarlett went along for the ride.

If she stayed in Cowboy Creek, she'd be letting Marianne make her choices for her again. But she wasn't sure she could leave. Marianne was her best friend. Life without her would be like losing an arm or an eye. She was beginning to think she didn't want to lose Travis either. He wanted a helpmeet, a partner. She didn't know if she could be that. She might do just fine out here. She hadn't lied when she told him she felt stronger every day. She could live to a ripe old age.

Or not. Only time would tell. How much time was Travis willing to give her to find out?

Chapter Eight

"**M**arianne!"

Ignoring the startled glances from the other women crowded into the small kitchen, Scarlett wove a path around furniture and skirts to embrace her sister. Tears filled both women's eyes as they laughed and hugged. It had only been a week and a half since Scarlett had seen Marianne, but it felt like a lifetime. Their lives had changed in ways Scarlett never expected when she and Marianne boarded that first train to Louisville last month.

"I wasn't sure you'd be here," Marianne said. "I was afraid to get my hopes up."

Scarlett squeezed her harder. "Where else would I be? Marla said there was work to be done, and this was what we were doing. She didn't give me much choice."

Marianne laughed. "That sounds like Marla."

"I would've come regardless," Scarlett assured her.

Not just her and Marianne but everyone in Cowboy Creek, she realized. Everyone pitched in to help whenever and wherever the work was, regardless of one's personal situation. Like a large, extended, caring family. This was how Scarlett suspected a community was supposed to work. She just hadn't known what it looked like or if there was a place in it for her. As kind and generous as the people of Cowboy Creek were, none of them had the means or time to support a fragile woman who couldn't pull her weight.

"It's so good to see you," she told Marianne. "I almost don't know what to do without you."

"I feel the same way."

"Humph. With a new husband I'm sure you have plenty to do with yourself."

An uncharacteristic blush warmed Marianne's lovely features. "I suppose, but my whole life has been with you. This is wonderful," she gestured around the bustling room of women working together, "but different. A lot to get used to."

Scarlett wanted to ask about Nathan and married life and so many other questions that would've kept them whispering for hours back home. Such topics were taboo and couldn't be broached in a roomful of strangers. Work awaited. Long after the work was over, Nathan would be waiting for his wife. A pang of homesickness and melancholy struck Scarlett as she wondered if she and Marianne would ever again enjoy the close relationship they had growing up.

She pushed the melancholy aside. No time for feeling sorry for herself. During the ride to the Campbell cabin, Marla and Preach had explained the way things would work for the next few weeks. Since there were few laborers for hire in the area, the men had developed a system of helping each other with harvesting, calving, and whatever other chores the seasons brought. Depending on which homestead required attention first, the group moved from ranch to ranch to harvest the fields and take care of chores that couldn't be put off. With the added workforce of brides, the men could devote their energy to the fields and herds while the women fixed meals for the hungry workers and preserved food and supplies for the coming winter.

Marla took two tin cups out of a bag she had brought and held one out to Scarlett. "Let's have some coffee before we get started. The dampness out there has settled into these old bones."

Scarlett gratefully headed for the pot simmering on the stove. Dawn had barely cracked the sky when they drove away from the trading post that morning. Preach assured them of a warm, clear day, but that was hours away. Between cooking a mountain of food, the women would harvest and preserve the last of Rennie Campbell's late beans and squash, then turn the garden over by hand. Tomorrow the group would go through the whole process at another ranch until every field was harvested and every homestead winterized.

Marianne squeezed her elbow. "We'll have a chance to talk while we work later. I want to hear what you think of Cowboy Creek. And the people here."

Scarlett knew she meant Travis and if things were progressing between them. There was nothing to tell. She liked him and he seemed to like her back. None of that mattered, though, if she was too frail to become someone's bride, but she didn't want to admit it to Marianne.

She leaned into her sister's one-armed hug, careful to avoid burning her with the scalding coffee. "I'm looking forward to it."

After a few minutes with their coffee cups, the women set to work.

The morning passed rapidly. The women laughed and talked as they worked in teams, toting vegetables in from the garden, cooking food for the noon meal, or washing, peeling, and chopping the last of the vegetables for preserving.

Scarlett marveled at how quickly everything got done, considering this was the first time any of them had worked as a team on such a project. The light-hearted camaraderie filled her with gladness. These women acted like friends or sisters rather than a motley crew who'd only known each other a few months.

She was put to work outside at a bubbling tub of hot water, cleaning and scouring canning jars for meat they were cooking off the bone inside. The cool of the morning burned off, and she was soon hot and weary. At least she was outside where the steam from the water dissipated into the air. Still, it became harder and harder to fill her lungs with air. She tried to focus on the activity and laughter around her instead of how heavy her arms felt.

She set clean jars in a tub and carried them into the sweltering cabin. Heat hit her like a fist. Marianne stood at the sideboard with her back to the door shredding cooked chicken. Wisps of auburn hair clung to the back of her neck. Her arms moved rapidly as she worked, the way Scarlett had seen her do her whole life. All they'd ever known was hard work and lean times. Life here offered nothing more but the same. Marianne was up to the task. As for Scarlett, she just didn't know.

The oppressive heat pressed in on her chest like a hot, wet blanket. The jars in the heavy tub rattled together as she struggled to draw a deep breath. A cough formed in her chest and worked its way up her throat. She gulped at the humid air, willing the cough under control until she could set down the tub.

The cough bubbled forward. With shaking hands, she set the tub on the table too close to the edge of the table. The cough bubbled forth. She was too weak to steady the tub. It toppled to the floor. The crash of metal striking the floor and breaking glass thrust the cabin into stunned silence. Scarlett stood in a pool of broken glass and let the cough have its way. She clasped a hand over her mouth. She pressed her other arm across her chest to alleviate the pressure on her ribs as the cough shook her body all the way down to her trembling knees.

The women sprang into action, shouting commands to each other. Someone grabbed the upended tub and began putting the unbroken jars and largest pieces of glass into it. Someone else grabbed a broom. Another took Scarlett's arms and backed her out of the pool of shattered glass and toward the door. She couldn't resist or stand upright as the cough wracked her body.

In the fresh air, she was guided into a chair. Hands loosened her apron strings and the buttons of her bodice. She recognized the hands as Marianne's. Someone pushed a wet cloth into Marianne's hand. She bathed Scarlett's face and neck. The coughing slowly eased.

"I…I'm so…sorry," she managed, directing her words at her knees since she was too weak and breathless to look up. "All those jars…what a waste."

"Don't worry about the jars," Marianne said brusquely. "Just catch your breath."

Annie, Carrie's little girl, appeared at Marianne's side and held out a dipper of water. "Here you go, Miss Scarlett. Are you all right?"

Scarlett nodded and managed to smile as she took the dipper and drank gratefully.

"Can you fill it again, Annie?" Marianne asked. The little girl scampered off.

Scarlett sank against the back of the chair and put her hand on her chest. Her rapid heartbeat was disconcerting, though she knew it would slow down in a minute or two. It always did. She opened her eyes to see her sister's concerned face hovering over her.

Now that Marianne realized she would survive the bout of coughing, her jaw tightened. She set her hands on her hips. "All right, I want to know every word Doc Gaetz told you."

"He said what they always told the girls at the factories. Our lungs were overtaxed from breathing in those chemicals and fibers. Fresh air was the only hope we had."

She smiled weakly to alleviate the apprehension on Marianne's face. "Well, the air can't get much fresher than this. The kitchen was just so hot, and I was hurrying because I knew you were waiting for the jars. There's nothing more to it than that. Doc said I should avoid overworking in the heat. It was my own fault."

"Why didn't you tell anyone? You didn't have to wash every jar. We could've put you to work in the garden where you'd have a breeze. You could take a break any time."

Scarlett sat up straight. "You and none of the other women took breaks. Work has to be done, no matter how difficult or uncomfortable. I'll do my share."

"But you're sick. We understand you need time to recover."

Annie jumped back onto the porch and held out the dipper, dripping with fresh water.

Scarlett ignored the little girl. She kept her eyes on her sister. "I won't be pampered like a princess. I'm weaker and slower than the rest of you, but I will pull my weight. I won't sit in the shade while the rest of you do all the work."

"You're not telling me everything, Scarlett. I can tell. I want the whole story."

Scarlett heaved a sigh. "There's nothing to tell. You know how this works as well as I do. Many of the women who worked in the factories lived perfectly healthy lives. Others didn't. There's no way of knowing which one I'll be. I can't live my life like a china doll, afraid every coughing spell will be my last."

Marianne grabbed her hand. "Don't say that. Don't ever say that."

Scarlett put her free hand over Marianne's and patted it. "And please, don't baby me." She looked down at the little girl at her elbow, concern and confusion all over her upturned face. She took the dipper from her. "Thank you, sweetheart." She sipped it carefully.

Marianne pursed her lips and waited, clearly measuring her own words for the sake of the child. "Thank you, Annie," she said after Scarlett finished drinking. "You can go back to your brother now." The women watched her dash away. Marianne turned back to Scarlett. "I shouldn't have forced you to come here. The work's too much."

Scarlett raised her hand. "Stop! We've already settled this. If we'd stayed in the city, you wouldn't have met Nathan and all these wonderful people. Do you think I want that blame heaped on me?"

"That's not what I meant."

"Well, that's what I hear every time you tell me how you shouldn't have brought me because I'm too delicate. I'm not strong enough to handle what the rest of you handle without complaint. I don't need reminded. And I don't need mollycoddled. Let me figure out my limitations on my own. I am getting stronger. You may not see it, but I can tell. I'm here with you instead of lying in a hospital bed, aren't I? Stop bossing me around."

A smile curved Marianne's lips. "I keep doing that, don't I?"

Scarlett smiled back. "All. The. Time. You'll have babies soon and you can boss them around until they get big enough to outrun you." She glanced around. "Speaking of which…"

She took Marianne's hands and pulled her onto an upturned wooden crate. "I've never seen that flush on your face before. Married life must agree with you. Tell me about Nathan. Is he as sweet and kind as he is handsome? Have you gotten him to come out of his shell? When you first met, you were worried you'd never get two words out of him."

Marianne glanced over her shoulder to make sure no one else was within hearing. ""He's more than I ever thought I'd find in a husband. He is still quiet but strong. And intelligent. It's wonderful. He doesn't let me boss him around, I tell you that, though it doesn't stop me from trying. He'll always be a man of few words, but we're getting to know each other without talking all the time." Her blush deepened. "I can't wait until the same thing happens for you."

Scarlett didn't want to talk about herself. She wrapped her arms around Marianne's shoulders. "I miss you so much."

Marianne hugged her back. "I miss you, too, but we're neighbors. After harvest is over and you get settled, we'll have more time to spend together."

Scarlett pulled away. Would she ever be settled here and part of the community like Marianne? "I hope so. It's a different world than Cincinnati."

Marianne's face softened into a warm glow. "I have to admit it's not easy after living in the city where everything we needed was at our fingertips. Patience has never been my strong suit as you know. I guess I'll have to work on that. And contentment." She sighed. "But I'm so happy we came." She squeezed Scarlett's hands again. "I pray it works out for you the same as it has for me. This place filled an emptiness in me I didn't know I had. It feels like I'm home. Especially now that you're here."

"I'm glad we came too," Scarlett replied honestly, She looked out over the barnyard. In the distance came the sounds of men's voices. Inside the cabin and around the yard, the other women were back to work. A tub of broken jars wouldn't slow them down for long.

Marianne glanced over her shoulder at the open window. "I need to get back inside. I want you to stay right here and take advantage of this lovely breeze the Lord sent us." Scarlett opened her mouth to protest. Marianne sharply squeezed her knee, cutting her off. "You won't be of use to anyone if you wear yourself out. Sometime today we'll find a chance to talk again. I want to hear all about Travis."

Heat rushed to Scarlett's face. "What about him?"

Marianne laughed, a trilling, girlish sound that reminded Scarlett of their childhood before life got so hard. "Oh, I hear things, little sister, even all the way out at my and Nathan's place. I know he's spent time with you, and I can see on your face he's made an impression." She leaned forward to kiss Scarlett's cheek. "Please take it easy. When you feel up to it, find something to do outside. The men will be in soon, and they'll be hungry. Travis, too. We don't want you looking peaked and scaring him away."

Scarlett didn't comment. She watched Marianne go inside. No matter how long they lived she doubted she could keep anything from her sister. She pressed her hands to her chest and took a few deep breaths. She felt rattling under her hands. That couldn't be good. How bad was it? How many deep breaths did she have left?

Marianne would be disappointed if Scarlett told her she couldn't marry Travis. She expected Scarlett to find the same love, fulfillment, and security she had found with Nathan. She wouldn't understand such a life wasn't possible for everyone.

Chapter Nine

It was easy to stay true to her word and take it easy the rest of the day. Scarlett was too weak and depleted to do anything else. J.T. and Candace were in the garden struggling with hand tillers to turn the ground under for its winter rest. Candace was having some success. J.T.'s skinny arms strained from the effort. Annie followed behind busting up dirt clods with her gloved hands. Not especially productive, but it kept her occupied and out of the way.

Scarlett went to the well and pumped a bucket of water, then carried it back to the garden and sat on a log stump. Annie quickly joined her. When the other children were ready for a break, they sat around the stump and passed the dipper of cold water while Scarlett entertained them with stories. She wished she could do more of the heavy work, but she supposed keeping the children occupied was help in itself.

An hour later when Katie and Eliza came outside to set up sawhorses and sheets of plywood for the noon meal, Scarlett hurried over to help. She hoped they wouldn't mention her earlier trouble. The last thing she wanted was pity or for people to treat her more gently than anyone else. The women seemed to sense it. Eliza shoved a heavy stack of plates in her arms and told her where she could find the box of silverware inside.

A pleasant breeze ruffled the blankets covering the tables and dispersed the sun's heat. Scarlett breathed deeply of the clean, leaf-scented air as she hurried back and forth with crocks of food and laughed and talked with the women who were past ready for a break from their labors.

When the last dish was in place, Candace Whitamore stretched onto her toes to ring the dinner bell. The men trickled in from beyond the barn, smiling and joking among themselves as the women positioned themselves around the table. Despite the weeks of work ahead of them, the mood was light. Scarlett sought out Travis in the group. He wasn't hard to spot. He was obviously looking for her. Their gazes locked as the men veered in the direction of the horse trough to wash up. She ignored the flutter in her stomach. Before they left Cincinnati, Marianne told her a woman named Nan Canfield, Rase's aunt, had been responsible for matching each woman to the man who suited her best. From the looks on the married couples' faces the process had gone off without a hitch. Even Marianne and Nathan, who had not been matched by Miss Canfield, seemed perfectly suited. God must've been involved, preparing each heart for the one designed just for it.

What about Travis and her? Their interests and dispositions seemed suited, but she couldn't saddle him with a wife who couldn't give him the life he wanted.

During the meal the men sat at one end of the table discussing their progress and what was next on the agenda while the women sat at the other talking and laughing and enjoying the rare opportunity to discuss everything and nothing. When the food was gone, the men gushed their thanks and squeezed their wives before sauntering toward the barn, taking time to digest before rushing back to work. The women wrapped the crocks with towels and carried them into the cabin. The leftover food would be eaten tonight as a light supper before everyone went home and prepared to do the whole thing tomorrow at the next farm. Scarlett reached for a box of eating utensils. Travis's large hands wrapped around the box. "I'll get that."

Scarlett jerked back as if scalded. She pursed her lips to cover a giggle of embarrassment. "I didn't see you there."

He lifted the heavy box as if it weighed nothing. "So I gathered. You've been ignoring me all afternoon."

Scarlett opened her mouth to protest before she realized he was teasing. "Some of us have work to do."

"Not too much to say howdy, I'd think. A fella can get his feelings hurt pretty quick when a gal doesn't find time for that."

"I didn't realize your feelings were so fragile."

"Well, now you know."

Scarlett watched him for a moment. She wished she could think of something clever and witty to say in return. Despite working in the city all her life, she didn't have much experience with men. She didn't know what to expect from them except what she gleaned through friends who weren't much more successful in that department than she was.

Travis rattled the wooden box of utensils. "Where would you like this, please?"

"Oh, sorry. In the…um…" Why did he leave her so flustered? She grabbed a quilt off the table and rolled it in her arms. She hurried across the yard, but his long legs easily kept up with her. She reached for the door handle as it swung open. Bridget DeSantis held onto the other side.

Her tall, lean figure pulled up short in the doorway. Her gaze slid past Scarlett to Travis. "Why, Travis. I expected you to be back to work by now."

"The company's much more pleasurable here," he teased.

Bridget arched an eyebrow at Scarlett. "I suppose it is. Well, set that down. Scarlett will show you where. And make haste. If Eliza catches you lollygagging, she'll put you to work at the stove and you'll learn what real work looks like."

"I sure don't want that."

Bridget smiled at Scarlett before continuing outside. Scarlett set the rolled quilt on the pile in a rocking chair and motioned Travis to the sink board on the other side of the room. Thankfully, the cabin was empty. It wouldn't stay that way for long. "Thank you," she said.

"No, thank you. Any chance to spend a little time with you is a pleasure for me."

She glanced at the smooth floor. Relieved of his burden, Travis took her hand. "I hope you're not overworking yourself. You look flushed. It sure is hot in here."

She trusted no one had told him about her accident with the canning jars. He needn't know the flush on her cheeks had nothing to do with the temperature inside the cabin or her fragile lungs. "I've been outside in the garden most of the morning. Probably got a little sun."

He wasn't buying it. He took her other hand and positioned her in front of him, toe to toe. "After the other day, I worry about you."

"Do you mean the day you helped me off the roof?" she asked, though she knew which day he meant.

"No, not that day."

She pulled her hands free. "I don't want anyone worrying about me. I'm…"

"Fine?" He took her chin with a gentle finger and thumb and brought her gaze up to his. "That's what you keep saying."

"Because I am."

His dark brows slid together. "I hope so."

Feminine footsteps sounded on the porch outside. Scarlett lengthened the distance between them. "Thank you for your help."

Travis glanced at the door. "Anytime, Miss Scarlett. And thank you for dinner. It was delicious." He tipped his hat at Carrie and Rennie as they entered. "Ladies."

They stopped talking at the sight of him. Rennie set her hands on her hips, the swell of motherhood unmistakable under her apron. "You still here underfoot, Travis Lindell? Did you forget the way to the barn?"

Travis combed a hand through his hair and set his hat on his head. Nonplussed by the teasing, he cast another glance at Scarlett before nodding to the other women and going outside, his heavy boots ringing on the floorboards. Scarlett pressed her lips together to keep from smiling, but she knew her feelings were written all over her face. What was she going to do about that man?

❀ ❀ ❀

It was nearly dark by the time the tired group lined up their wagons to load supplies and head home. Rennie and her husband Jacob moved from wagon to wagon, thanking everyone for coming, though they'd be helping someone else tomorrow. Scarlett was exhausted. The work she did at the laundry was difficult and taxing, but today had drained her. She watched the other women laughing and talking as if they hadn't worked their fingers to the bone all day. She wanted to be useful like them—a benefit to the community. Instead, she just wanted to go home and fall into her bed. If Dr. Gaetz were here, he would tell her to stay at the brides' house tomorrow and rest. She was tempted to do exactly that, but she couldn't. She would do her share even if it…

She pushed the thought aside before it could take shape. She looked through the deepening shadows for Travis. He had been too busy to exchange more than a passing nod and a smile as they filled their plates during their supper of leftovers. There had been little talking between anyone. Everyone was anxious to get back to work to beat the darkness.

She hefted a sawhorse into the back of Preach's wagon. Marla appeared and grabbed the legs to help her swing it into the wagon bed. Travis and Lonnie Fanshaw pushed through the darkness, toting a sheet of lumber between them. They slid it on its end into the wagon. "Here's the last of everything, Marla."

Marla stepped out of the way as the men adjusted the load for an easier pull for the horses. Lonnie tipped his hat at Scarlett and Marla and faded into the night. The blacksmith hadn't uttered more than a handful of words to her since she arrived, though she often heard his jovial voice and laugh ring out while talking with the men. She wondered if he would find a bride. He was older than the others; tall and gawky and rather awkward looking. She hoped there was a woman on her way to Cowboy Creek who would put a light in his faded eyes.

Travis clapped his hands together, dispelling her musing about the blacksmith. "Looks like the wagon's full up." He turned to Scarlett. "Guess you'll have to ride with me."

Scarlett looked from Marla to Travis. "If you're sure it's not an inconvenience. It's out of your way."

Travis laughed easily. "Everywhere is out of everyone's way around here."

"He's right," Marla interjected. "You'll never fit in here with Daniel and me. You go on ahead. These old bones are tired. I'm ready to drop straight into bed. We're not even going to unload the wagon. Good night to both of you." She headed around the front of the wagon to find her husband.

Travis took Scarlett's elbow and guided her to his rig parked on the other side of the barn. "Let's hurry so we can get in front of Preach and Marla. They'll be moving slow. Knowing Preach, he'll want to ride side by side and talk the whole way. I'd rather talk to you."

A giggle escaped Scarlett's throat as she let him propel her into the darkness. She felt like they were doing something naughty. She was glad for the darkness so he couldn't see the flush in her cheeks.

Once they were seated, he held the reins easily, allowing the horse to pick its way around the ruts and dips of the road in the darkness. "Marla seems to enjoy playing matchmaker," Scarlett said after a few moments of dipping and swaying with the wagon.

Travis laughed. "She's been doing it since the first of you showed up. Having all you brides—er, ladies—here has been a balm to her soul. I never thought about how lonely it must've been for her with no women around. I think that's why most of the families left as soon as the ore played out. The men wanted money, and the women—what few there were—couldn't bear the isolation."

She looked around the landscape. "It is quiet. And lonely."

"It can be, I'll give you that. We men are hankering to build up a regular community. We want to leave something for the next generation. Jesus called his disciples to produce fruit, and he told them their fruit would remain after they were gone. He didn't call any of us for Heaven. We've got work to do here on earth. I guess it's to love people and help them and leave something that makes things better for the next ones."

Scarlett toyed with the ends of her shawl. "I never really thought much about what I'm doing on earth. Except to work and earn enough to feed Marianne and me for another day."

"That's pretty much as far as most of us have the luxury of thinking. Life's got to be more than that, though, don't you think? The disciples had plenty of work to do. They had to eat and support their families, but they were also given the job of spreading a whole new way of thinking throughout the world. I don't think God expects me to travel the whole world, but it is my responsibility to do what I can right here where He planted me."

Scarlett's eyes widened. "You sound like a preacher."

Travis scratched the bristle on his chin. "I reckon I do sometimes. Guess it's Preach rubbing off on me. I didn't get much Bible learning when I was coming up. I didn't even see a Bible until I was about ten or twelve. I never heard the word *Jesus* when I was a boy unless somebody was using it as a swear word."

Scarlett couldn't imagine anyone not knowing the word *Jesus,* but she didn't interrupt.

"A group of folks had set up a little stage outside of our town and set a piano on it. All week long, I listened to somebody torturing that piano and the whole group singing. They sure were having a time. In between the singing I heard this booming voice hollering about something. I was far away to tell what he was saying, but he sure was wound up about it, and it sounded important.

"Finally, my curiosity got the better of me. It was about half dark when I sneaked into the back of the crowd and listened for a while. I didn't understand much of what that preacher man was going on about, but every person there was hanging on his every word. I figured I better, too, if I knew what was good for me. Like I said, I didn't know Jesus was a real person or that He knew anything about me. I sure didn't know He loved me. How could He if He knew so much and knew where I lived—er, where I came from?"

His voice cracked. He looked at Scarlett, almost apologetically, as if he hadn't meant to say so much. Scarlett stared. She'd never heard a man speak so passionately about his relationship with the Lord. She didn't even know men had thoughts like that, except for maybe preachers, and it was their job to think that way.

"I gave my life to the Lord that night. I wasn't sure at the time what it meant. I just wanted whatever it was that got that preacher man and all those people at that meeting so fired up. When I got home I didn't tell nobody. Like I said I wasn't even sure what had happened. I found a beat-up Bible in one of the rooms and started reading it. I didn't have much education, so it didn't make a lot of sense, but I couldn't stop reading. I guess some of it got through my thick head. My life was never the same."

Scarlett's heart pricked. She'd read the Bible some when she had time. She attended church meetings as often as she could, but she never thought much about how doing so could change her life or who she was.

"Was your mother a maid in the hotel?"

He gave her a startled look. "Excuse me?"

"The hotel where you lived. You said you found a Bible in one of the rooms. You talked about different types of people coming in and out of your life. I didn't mean to make assumptions. I just thought you lived in a hotel and your ma was a maid or something."

A muscle twitched in Travis's chiseled jaw.

"It's nothing to be ashamed of," she said softly. "Women often have to take jobs they'd rather not to keep food on the table. That's what happened with Marianne and me. I'm sure it was doubly hard for your ma with a child and no man to help carry the load."

He gave her a quick glance, his cinnamon eyes hooded. "It was, especially after she took sick."

Scarlett wasn't sure what she'd said wrong. They'd been having a nice conversation. Now he barely looked at her. He hadn't wanted to talk about his pa either when she asked where he'd learned the woodworking trade. Losing his parents at such a young age still weighed grievously on him.

She shouldn't have asked such thoughtless questions about things that were none of her business. Travis was so forthcoming and at ease about most things. His parents were obviously the one topic he didn't want to talk about. She placed her hand on his and squeezed.

Chapter Ten

He said too much. He had talked too much about growing up in Kansas and piqued Scarlett's curiosity, so she needed to ask clarifying questions. He could just go with it. Let her think his mother was a maid, which would be a lot simpler than explaining what she really did.

In a way Mama was a maid. The girls who worked above the saloon had plenty of other duties besides showing the cowboys and businessmen in town a good time. They served drinks. They played the piano and sang and danced. They took turns working in the kitchen, and they all did their share of housekeeping and running errands for Mr. Keplinger.

When Scarlett set her hand on his, Travis nearly squeezed hers in return and let her think whatever she wanted. That would be a lie. Mama may have done a maid's work, but she wasn't a maid. The respectable women of Lawrence didn't cross to the other side of the street when they saw a maid coming. They didn't stop talking when a maid walked into a store and refused to look her in the eye or tipped their noses toward the ceiling as if they smelled something repugnant.

He needed to just tell her. He was sorry he hadn't been clear enough. His mama didn't work as a maid. She was a painted lady who worked above a saloon and wore dresses with her bosom hanging out, and pretended those looks from the respectable women in town didn't tear her heart out. His pa hadn't died a hero on a battlefield or from a tragic sickness or accident. For all Travis knew, his father was still alive somewhere. A businessman perhaps. Or a lawman. A bow-legged cowboy or toothless prospector. God only knew. It wasn't likely Mama did, though she claimed Travis looked just like the man. It was probably another of her candy-coated lies she repeated so he'd stop asking questions.

Travis was a coward. He had left Lawrence, Kansas to get away from those judgmental looks. No one in Cowboy Creek knew he was a product of those smoke-filled, sin-filled saloons where men went to throw away their money and destroy their marriages with the nameless, moral-less women who lived upstairs. He couldn't tell Scarlett any of that. He liked her, and he didn't want to ruin things between them. If he saw the look on her face those respectable ladies directed at Mama, it would break his heart. He wasn't ready to take the chance.

"I'm not ashamed of my ma," he replied honestly. "She worked hard. After she got sick and couldn't do as much, she made sure there were others to take care of me. She spread the word that I needed work so I could earn a few coins. The people around us were helpful to her and kind to me."

"It sounds like they were good people."

If only she knew.

For all the shame that came with his upbringing, he had an easier time coming up than some men he knew who had a ma and a pa of good standing at home. He'd heard plenty of stories about what went on behind the doors of those reputable homes that would turn Scarlett's hair white.

"After Mama died, I stayed in Lawrence for a few years. Nobody wanted to put me in the orphan's home. That wasn't a good situation for anyone, and I was nearly at the point where I could take care of myself anyway. Mr. Keplinger put me to work sweeping up and running errands and mucking after the horses. I slept above the stables most nights when the weather cooperated.

"It wasn't a bad life. There's always work around town for a boy with a strong back. Men at the feed mill would throw me coins for loading their wagons or bringing them a cart of firewood. Sometimes I took farm work or logging. Let me tell you, if the farmer had a wife, the eating sure was better than if he didn't."

Scarlett smiled in response.

"A lot of terrible things can happen to a boy without a family. Sometimes they did happen. Even then, I was always taken care of. Just when I'd get filled with despair, someone somewhere would do me a kindness. Once a lady from a church came and gave me a sack of old clothes she said her boy had outgrown. Those were the nicest, warmest clothes I ever put on. Not a worn place or hole or patch anywhere. I don't know how she knew about me or that I was cold and all my clothes were threadbare and so small I could barely fasten them around me. I never saw that lady again. Sometimes I wondered if she was a real or some sort of angel the Lord sent to provide for me. Those clothes were sure real enough, though."

The wagon hit a rut, rattling the tools in the wagon bed. Scarlett jostled against him. Travis put his arm around her to steady her. He considered leaving it there. She was so soft and warm. He wanted to kiss her. Hold her the rest of the way to the brides' house. Reluctantly, he lowered his arm.

"After I heard that preacher man and tried living different than what I always had, I felt a heaviness in my heart that I wasn't where God meant for me to be. It was almost like He was whispering in my ear that if I stayed in Lawrence, I'd end up like most of the men I knew there. Drinking every night. Shoving my woman around. Never having money in my pocket or amounting to anything. I started thinking God had something better in store for me."

Talking about God was easier than talking and thinking about Mama and the life they lived in Kansas. Scarlett smiled from beneath the brim of her straw hat. "I like the idea of God caring enough for me to whisper in my ear that He had something good in store for me."

"Now, you know I didn't actually mean He was talking in my ear."

"Oh, I know. You just sensed His presence and His…love for you."

"Yes. Love." The reins went slack in Travis's hands as he stared at her. He could barely see the outline of her face in the darkness. Her smooth brow, the slope of her cheek. He couldn't see the light in her blue eyes, but he knew she was looking back at him just as intently. He slowly brought his hand up and cupped her cheek. Just as he thought, her skin was as soft as velvet under his fingers. He felt as much as heard a delicate intake of breath. He leaned toward her, anticipating the thrill of her lips against his.

A tiny cough escaped her throat. She jerked her head away from his and coughed again. Louder and harder. She tried to suppress it, but her body went rigid as the cough rolled out of her, wave after wave. They weren't stopping. She fumbled for the handkerchief in her sleeve and clapped it over her mouth.

It took a heartbeat for Travis to react. He jerked the horse to a stop and dug for the canteen in the box behind him. A little water sloshed inside it as he wrestled to get the lid off. He hoped there was enough. He held the canteen in front of her face, but she couldn't stop coughing long enough to take a sip. He yanked his kerchief from around his neck and poured a little of the precious water over it. Why hadn't he taken the time to fill the canteen before he left the Campbells'? He dabbed her forehead with the damp kerchief. She turned away from him in the seat and bent nearly double as the cough continued.

Fear gripped his chest. What was happening? Was she going to die right in front of him? He glanced behind him, hoping to catch sight of Preach and Marla coming up behind them. They'd know what to do. At least they'd know more than he did.

He leaped to his feet on the narrow floorboard and climbed over Scarlett. He dropped to the ground and pulled her down beside him. She tried to bend over again, but he forced her to stand upright. When he was a kid, his ma always told him to raise his arms over his head when he coughed. He never understood why, but it usually worked. He lifted Scarlett's arms and rested them on his shoulders.

Within seconds the cough subsided. She sagged against him. Her entire body trembled. From fatigue, most likely, and possibly fear as well. He helped her sit, then handed her the canteen. This time she took a careful drink, then another.

Now that the threat of imminent death had passed, Travis's fear turned to anger. "Scarlett, what was that? I thought—" He raked his hand through his hair. "I didn't know if…" He swallowed hard to stop his voice from shaking.

"It was…I'm fine," she managed. "The dirt from the road, it got in my throat. That's all."

He sank to the ground beside her to look her in the eye. "Don't give me that. There's hardly any dust in the air tonight. You're either not telling me what's going on or the doc didn't tell you."

Scarlett took another drink of water, emptying the canteen, then drew a shaky breath. "Travis, I promise, there's nothing to tell. It was a long day. I probably overdid it in the garden."

Some of the aggravation leaked out of him, though he was sure she wasn't being completely truthful. "Maybe you shouldn't come tomorrow. Everyone will understand—"

She grabbed his arm. "No! I'm not going to sit in the shade like an old lady and watch everyone else work. I did enough of that today."

"Scarlett—"

"I said, no. And I don't want you telling anyone about this either. I just overtaxed myself."

He looked past her into the darkness. She wasn't telling him the truth. Just like Mama. She didn't know him that well. Maybe she wasn't comfortable enough with him to tell her secrets. The Lord knew he hadn't told her all of his.

"Does Doc Gaetz know how bad your cough gets?"

"Honestly, Travis, it could've been much worse. You should've seen the girls in the factories. Sometimes they'd cough up a ball of lint like a cat."

"And what became of them? Are they still working in those conditions?"

It was her turn to look away. "Well, mostly no. But we're not talking about them. I'm out of that terrible laundry. Hopefully every day will get better."

"And if it doesn't?"

"Then it's in God's hands, isn't it?"

His chest tightened. He cared about her. He didn't know if he loved her yet, but he was headed in that direction. He was pretty sure she was going that way, too. Did he have it in him to love a woman he could lose at any moment? Watching her cough and labor for her next breath was something he never wanted to see again.

Scarlett brushed her hands off on the front of her skirt and started to stand. Travis jumped to his feet and took her hands to help her up. She smiled softly. She was close enough he smelled a hint of lemon in her hair. Her hands were so small and soft. He wanted to wrap his arms around her and pull her close. Finish the kiss he had nearly gotten earlier.

Instead, he turned her toward the wagon and helped her in. He couldn't think of much to say the rest of the way to the brides' house. Scarlett picked up on his mood and didn't talk either. Or she was just too exhausted for conversation. He wasn't sure which.

He knew it was too late to stop himself from falling for her. At the same time, he didn't know how close he wanted to get to a woman who didn't trust him enough to tell him the truth. What if she never did?

Chapter Eleven

Every night Scarlett fell into bed, tired and sore, but happy and content that another day was behind her. She couldn't bear the heat of the cabins, but she found other ways to contribute with the workload outside. Even if she couldn't work as hard as the other women, she knew she was a great help by minding the children and keeping them busy and out from underfoot. Still, she wished she could do more.

One afternoon while playing in the tall grass alongside the garden, Annie let out a scream that sent prickles of alarm down Scarlett's spine. She raced over to find the child frozen in fear within striking distance of a thick-bodied snake. Without pause, Scarlett lunged and chopped off the snake's head with her hoe. The cabin emptied as women came running to see what happened. Travis and Rase Canfield, who had been working the closest, heard the child's screams and hurried from the outbuildings.

Scarlett pointed a shaking finger. Now that the snake was dead, she couldn't find her voice. The men approached cautiously even though the snake was clearly dead. Dead snakes could strike in their death throes, so it was best to exercise caution. Annie cried and threw herself into her mother's arms. Even curious J.T. hung back.

Rase took the hoe from Scarlett and raised the snake aloft. "It's just a harmless ole' bull snake, and not a very big one," he announced.

"I thought it was a rattler," Scarlett said around a tight throat.

"It's an easy enough mistake to make, especially when you're not used to them."

While Rase urged the children to stay out of the high grass and showed them and the women the clear differences in venomous and non-venomous snakes, Travis put his arm over Scarlett's shoulders. "Are you all right?"

She nodded, then smiled sheepishly. "No."

He chuckled. "First year I was here I stomped the guts out of every snake I saw until I calmed down long enough to take a second look. There aren't nearly as many venomous snakes around these parts as you'd think. Best to assume they're all poisonous anyway and avoid them as much as you can until you learn the difference."

J.T. ran a cautious finger down the snake's still underbelly. "Can I keep him?"

"Ewww. Nooo!" Annie shrieked.

"Maybe your pappy will skin him for you, and you can nail his hide on the barn wall," Rase said.

J.T.'s eyes went round with excitement.

Annie's face turned purple with fear. "No! No! No!" she wailed. "Don't let 'im, Mama. Please, don't let him. I'll have bad dreams."

Carrie stroked the sobbing girl's head. "Looks like the answer's no, J.T. Maybe if there's a next time and she's a little older." She carried Annie to the cabin, murmuring soothing words as she went.

J.T. kicked at a clot of dried grass. Rase set a big hand on his shoulder. "Go get the shovel and we'll take this fella and his head and throw him over the hill."

Everyone else went back to work. Scarlett reached for the hoe Rase had left on the ground. She was dismayed to see her hand still shook. Travis took it from her and turned her toward the well. "How about we take a break."

She cast one last glance at the trampled grass. The snake could've just as easily been venomous. What if it was and she hadn't been armed with a hoe? This place could be so dangerous. More so for women and children. She shivered and allowed Travis to pull her against his side as they walked.

She perched on the side of the well. He drew up a bucket of cold water and offered her a dipperful.

"I don't know if I'll ever get used to this place," she said absently as she took the dipper from him.

"Do you mean that?"

She wished she hadn't spoken so quickly. "I don't know. I'm not sure I'm meant for the frontier. I'm not as strong as the other women and I'm a coward."

"A coward?" He laughed. "You took that snake's head off clean as a whistle."

She shuddered again. "Maybe so, but I'll never sit down outside or move a rock or hunk of wood again without looking twice."

"That's a good idea, no matter where you are."

She lowered the dipper and glared playfully. "Are you making fun of me?"

"I'm agreeing with you." He smiled. "You know there's danger no matter where you live."

"But not snakes," she insisted. "At least not that big."

He took hold of her dress sleeve and tugged. "What if I promise to protect you?"

Warmth flooded her face. "I suppose that'll help."

His smile faded as if he wished he hadn't been so glib. He took the dipper and took a deep drink. He hung it back on the nail and stood. "Guess I ought'a get back to work."

Scarlett sighed inwardly, missing him already though he was still standing next to her. He hadn't paid her much attention since the night she had her coughing fit on the way home from the Campbells'. She had about reached the conclusion he finally realized he needed a hardier woman than her with whom to share a life. If that were the case, he wouldn't have promised to protect her a minute ago. Her thoughts were so muddled. She liked Travis and enjoyed getting to know him. At the same time, she was better off not falling in love with this man. If only her heart would see reason.

Rase and J.T. came into view at the edge of the field. Without a word or glance in her direction, Travis walked away. When J.T. drew abreast of him dragging the shovel, J.T. spoke to him, but Travis barely took notice. Heaviness settled in Scarlett's stomach and lingered there the rest of the day. She tried to convince herself she didn't want Travis's attention, but she sure missed it when it was gone.

At the noon meal conversation focused on Scarlett's quick reaction to the snake, even though she'd needlessly killed a harmless bull snake. Jacob Campbell suggested she order a pair of glasses from one of the catalogs they stocked in Good Hope so she wouldn't make the mistake again. Scarlett laughed along with the others. Her gaze sought out Travis at the far end of the table. He was the only one at the table who didn't join in the teasing. She caught Marianne studying her. Her dark eyes questioned. Scarlett pretended not to notice.

As the men pushed away from the table—once again thanking their wives for the hearty fare and stealing quick hugs and kisses—clouds scudded across the sky and obscured the sun. The temperature dropped by several degrees.

Everyone looked skyward. "Looks like our workday is about to be cut short," Lonnie Fanshaw said. "We better hustle back to the fields if we want to finish anything." He was the only man who didn't benefit by sharing the field work as he didn't farm himself, save a small garden behind his house. Still, he would prosper as long as the farmers of Cowboy Creek had a good harvest.

Scarlett pushed thoughts of Travis out of her head as the men rushed back to work and the women hurriedly rolled the blankets they used to cover the tables and stowed the crocks of leftover food in the kitchen of the Waring house. Barely an hour passed when a rumble of thunder rolled across the prairie. Scarlett told the children to put away their gardening tools. A storm was about to descend upon them. She had just secured the door of the shed when the men came out of the fields. "That storm is going to be a real humdinger," Whit Whitamore called over the increasing wind. "Get your ma. We're heading home early today."

The children cheered and ran toward the house. Scarlett sought out Travis in the group. While part of her looked forward to a leisurely afternoon of sitting in her little house, reading or knitting or napping, she didn't look forward to a day without seeing him, even if he hadn't been as talkative of late.

Women poured out of the house to verify with their husbands that work was finished for the day. A flurry of activity followed as everyone gathered their things. Scarlett kissed Marianne goodbye and grabbed her wrap. With a few long strides, Travis left his loaded buckboard and reached for the basket she had brought.

Scarlett tightened her wrap around her head. "It's just up the road. I'll make a dash for it."

"No need," he said rather brusquely. "I have to go right past there. It'll save you a few raindrops."

Scarlett tensed, unsure of what to do. She wanted to accept the ride. She'd missed him the last few days, but this invitation wasn't like the ones before. There was no lighthearted playfulness in his cinnamon brown eyes. Only curt impatience. He took her elbow and turned her toward the buckboard. She stiffened. "I'll go with Marla and Preach."

"They've already gone. Come on. We're about to get soaked."

Tears smarted in Scarlett's eyes. This was what she wanted, wasn't it? For him to give up pursuing her and find a more suitable mate. When the harvest was over, she could move to Ruby City or another town where she could find work to support herself. The only one to miss her was Marianne, and Marianne would be busy and distracted with babies soon enough. She'd get used to not having Scarlett around in no time.

Out on the porch, the group listened to a crack of thunder much closer than the first. "You're all welcome to stay here and wait out the storm," Eliza told the group as heavy raindrops pelted the ground.

"Thanks anyway, but we'll get on our way," Sawyer Jamison answered. He took Katie's hand and the two of them hurried across the yard.

Travis tightened his grip on Scarlett's arm. The deliciously cool breeze grabbed at his hat and the ends of Scarlett's shawl. She clutched the shawl together at her throat with one hand and held onto Travis with the other. She was barely settled in the buckboard seat when Travis tapped the horse's flank and they were jostled forward. Fat raindrops landed on her cheeks and the tip of her nose. She hunched her shoulders and pulled her hat low around her ears.

"Don't worry, I'll get you home in a hurry." Travis handed her the reins, then reached behind her and pulled a large tarp around their shoulders. He barely got it adjusted before the rain began to fall in earnest.

Scarlett gripped the tarp and held it in front of her, creating shelter for their heads and faces while Travis guided the horse. A bolt of lightning pierced the sky, followed by a rumble of thunder. The horse whinnied and sidestepped away from the sound. Travis called out a command and straightened the path. Within a few minutes they reached the brides' house. Travis brought the buckboard to a stop under the overhang which was just big enough to shelter them from the rain. Scarlett jumped down and opened the front door. Travis grabbed her basket and followed her inside. He slapped his hat against his leg, sending a shower of raindrops into the room. Scarlett went straight to the stove and lit the paper and kindling chips she had laid out this morning.

"The storm sure came up quick."

"That's how it generally works out here."

A rumble of thunder shook the eaves above her head. "Would you like to stay for a cup of coffee? Perhaps the rain will let up."

"I think we're past that. I need to get the horse and wagon out of the storm."

She closed the stove lid and followed him to the door. "Thank you for the ride. You spared me from a muddy walk in the rain. Now you'll be the one soaked by the time you get home."

He reached for the door handle. Scarlett caught his sleeve. "Travis, is everything all right?"

He glanced at the ceiling. "I'm sure the roof'll keep you dry tonight. Might find a few new leaks."

"No. Not that. You. And me. I get the feeling I offended you the other day. I hope you know I consider you a friend."

"A friend? I got enough friends." He wrapped one arm around her and jerked her against him. He lowered his mouth to hers and kissed her. Scarlett's breath caught in her throat. She barely had time to respond before he let go of her so fast she stumbled. He stepped into the rain and jumped into the rig. He rode off without looking back. Off balance, Scarlett watched until the wagon disappeared from view, its wheels throwing rooster tails of muddy water into the night.

Chapter Twelve

Scarlett lay in bed and listened to the rain rat-a-tatting on the roof. Every few minutes she put her fingers to her lips, remembering Travis's kiss. Even before he pulled her into his arms, she wanted the kiss as much as he did. Maybe more. But now she didn't know if she was thrilled or disappointed. Thrilled that he had finally taken her in his arms. Disappointed that the kiss was not what she expected. What exactly had she expected? Desire, maybe. Tenderness. Instead, he had been almost...angry. As if he had a point to prove. She just wasn't sure what the point was.

He had barely spoken to her since the night they left the Campbell farm. She *had* offended him. But how? She didn't think he was mad because he witnessed how compromised her health was. He wasn't that kind of man. But he had pulled away. Had the same thing that occurred to her occurred to him? That they could never marry. He deserved a wife who could give him the life he wanted.

She rolled over and willed herself to go to sleep. This wasn't a problem she could solve. Things were the way they would always be.

Even though the rain would keep everyone out of the fields tomorrow, she knew there'd be plenty to keep her busy. Marla and Preach needed to inventory the trading post and pack items to take to Ruby City for bartering and trading. Helping Marla would be easier on Scarlett's constitution and would help keep her mind off Travis and his angry kiss.

It was still dark when she awoke but quiet out. The storm had moved on. It had also settled the dust and pollen in the air, clearing her lungs and leaving her energetic despite the poor night's sleep. In the next room, mice feet scattered into the shadows as she climbed out of bed. She'd done everything she could to rid the little house of the annoying critters, but still they found their way inside. Next time she saw a snake she wouldn't be so quick to chop its head off since it was her greatest ally in keeping the mice out of the larder.

At breakfast Preach told the women he and a few other men were spending the day with Whit at the mill to get it ready for the influx of work next week as everyone prepared for the trip to Ruby City. Scarlett wanted to ask if Travis would be among the men coming to help. She wanted to see him. She wanted to ask about his kiss. She wanted to know what he was thinking about her. At the same time, she doubted she would have the nerve to ask him anything. It was just as well if he was through pursuing her. When the group went to Ruby City she would stay there. She'd find a job her frail body could handle or move on to Denver or St. Louis where opportunities for a woman like her would be greater.

Either way, she didn't need to worry about what was behind Travis's kiss or if he planned to do it again.

She spent the morning with Marla, cleaning and catching up on chores they'd missed throughout the week. Every time a horse rode past on its way to the mill, Scarlett had to force herself not to run to the window to see if it was Travis. She wasn't looking forward to leaving Cowboy Creek and the friendships she'd forged with the other women. But there was no place for her here. The sooner she—and Travis—accepted it, the better.

Marla kept up a steady stream of conversation. Everyone loved and respected Marla, and it hadn't taken Scarlett long to figure out why. The older woman was like a mother or aunt she'd never had. Besides Marianne and Travis, she would miss Marla most of all.

This morning, she could barely focus on anything the older woman said, not that it mattered. Marla was quite content carrying the conversation on her own.

At noon she hitched Marla's mule to the buggy and drove to the mill to help Carrie prepare food for the workers. On an ordinary day they would've walked the short distance, but it was too far to carry the baskets loaded with food.

As soon as the younger children saw the buggy, they ran out to meet them. Scarlett's nose prickled with tears. Here were two more people she had grown to love that she'd probably never see again once she left Cowboy Creek.

Inside the house, Carrie and Marla assured her they could handle the work in the kitchen if she wanted to take the children outside. Scarlett preferred the fresh air over the stuffy kitchen any day of the week and let J.T. and Annie lead her out the door.

The children headed down the sloping ground to the creek. Scarlett stole a glance at the mill. No one was outside and she didn't hear voices over the roar of the water. It was moving faster than she had ever seen it. "Stay back from the water," she called out to the children. In response, they went even faster. Scarlett twisted her ankle on a round rock as she tried to keep up.

"We found a cave a few weeks ago over past that pile of rocks," J.T. said, pointing. "When the water goes down, we'll show you."

"It's a hidey hole for bandits," Annie exclaimed. "That's what J.T. said."

The boy's face turned red with indignation and embarrassment. "I did not."

"Yes, you did! You said bank robbers could've stashed their loot there, and one day we were going to find it."

He turned to Scarlett. "I was just funning her. She believes anything you tell her. The cave's not very big. Not even big as me. But someday we're gonna get in there and see if it ever got used for anything besides the badgers."

"You shouldn't fool around near the creek without telling your pa first. Those miners did a lot of digging and could've created weak spots that could be dangerous."

"Yes, ma'am." J.T. looked solemn. Annie had lost interest in the conversation and wandered farther down the path.

Scarlett knew her lecture was as useful as talking to a fencepost. As soon as they got the chance, the children would investigate the outcropping and imagine all sorts of fascinating tales about what may have happened there. She would've done the same thing as a child, especially here where their only playmates were nature and their own imaginations.

J.T. ran in the direction of a bent tree with limbs perfect for climbing. She opened her mouth to tell him to be careful but checked herself. Telling a boy not to climb a tree was like telling a bird not to chirp. She'd be tempted to climb up beside him if she wasn't afraid the other adults would see. Annie continued along the path, skipping and kicking rocks and singing to herself. Leaves had fallen and covered the ground. They were wet from yesterday's rain and slippery under Scarlett's shoes. The soles were thin and as slick as a duck's back. Before long she'd notice the cold ground through them. She couldn't imagine wearing them in deep snow. She and Marianne had spent nearly all their money coming west. She wasn't sure she could afford new shoes, especially with setting herself up in Ruby City or wherever she ended up. How would this work out? She needed to talk to Marianne about shoes and woolen underwear and everything else she'd need before winter set in.

"Miss Scarlett, look," Annie called from near the creek's edge.

Scarlett whipped her head toward Annie's voice. *How had the child gotten so close to the water?* That's what she got for woolgathering. "Annie, get back please."

"Look! This leaf's as big as my head." The little girl held up the large leaf for Scarlett to see, then put it on her head. A gust of wind snatched the leaf out of her hand.

The next moment happened so quickly Scarlett didn't have time to react. Annie grasped for the leaf as it blew out over the water. The mud on the bank gave way under her and she slipped into the rushing creek. The water wasn't more than a foot deep, but it was moving fast. Too fast for the little girl to get her legs under her before she was swept away.

"Annie!"

The force of the water turned Annie in a complete circle. "Mama!" she cried, her voice between a plaintive plea and a cry for help. Her eyes were as wide as teacups and her face white from fright against her dark hair.

"Mama!" she managed before the water upended her and dunked her face below the water's surface.

"Annie! Oh, God, help!"

Scarlett's feet finally unrooted from where she stood on the path. Annie's face popped up out of the water. Her skirt billowed around her shoulders, keeping her face out of the water. It also created a sail that carried her away from the water's edge into the deeper part of the creek. Scarlett knew this area of the creek had several pools of water five or six feet deep where the men cooled themselves in the summer. After the last month of ample rain, she could only imagine the power under the surface of the water.

Her lungs burned and heart raced as she slipped and slid along the wet, muddy bank. Annie spun out of reach. Her skirt soaked through and no longer held her upright.

"Oh, Jesus, help her," Scarlett said aloud as she ran.

As she uttered the words, Annie's skirt tangled in a clutch of brush and debris and stopped her progress. "Hold on," Scarlett called out to her, knowing even as she spoke, the words were pointless. Annie couldn't do anything but what the water dictated.

Scarlett reached the debris and fallen limbs and threw herself into the water. She climbed across the limbs through the water, her toes barely brushing the slippery bottom. "Hold on!"

Annie turned her terrified gaze to Scarlett but couldn't speak around the sobs that wracked her body. Branches clawed at Scarlett's clothes. The inside of her calf sliced open against something sharp under the water. Fear and cold numbed the pain. With all the energy she could muster, she lunged at the child. Her hand closed around a piece of Annie's dress. She tried to pull Annie toward her, but her frozen fingers wouldn't cooperate. Her lungs burned. Her arms felt weighted down and useless. She tried to kick closer, but her own dress was tangled in the branches. She couldn't risk letting go of Annie to free herself.

"Help me!" she cried again to God or the branches or even Annie. The roar of water filled her ears. Water washed over Annie's head. Her mouth opened and closed, reminding Scarlett of a fish on a dock, gasping for air and fright and not knowing what to do.

"I've…got…you…" Scarlett gasped as she pulled closer. A seam somewhere in her dress tore loose and she was able to get a better grip on Annie's skirt. If only she could reach Annie's arm or shoulder. The water pulled harder as though trying to break Scarlett's hold.

Annie's face went under the water again. "Mama!" she screamed when she bobbed up before the water took her under again.

Scarlett grunted and kicked at the debris holding her. If she could get closer, she could grab the top half of Annie to keep her head out of the water. Her foot found a tree root. She braced against it and stretched as far as she could. The icy water pulled at her, zapping her strength. If not for getting caught in the debris, she and Annie would both be pulled farther from the creek's edge.

She couldn't hold Annie's dress much longer. Her fingers had lost their feeling, and her arms had no strength. Water pulled steadily at her. Her chest felt like someone had put a hundred-pound weight on it. With the last of her strength, she lunged forward to wrap her arm around the child. She lost her foothold under the water and missed. Annie was swept away from her completely.

Scarlett opened her mouth to scream but nothing came out. She watched in silent terror as Annie hurtled down the stream away . Scarlett yanked her dress free from the debris and let the water carry her spinning and rolling after Annie. She wanted to pray, but all she could focus on were breathing and keeping Annie in sight. She didn't know what she'd do once she caught hold of the child. The water was in control.

Her heart pounded. Her lungs felt ready to explode. Her arms and legs were useless against the rushing water.

She saw a dense thicket of trees ahead of them. A low branch hung over the water and another section of debris had caught on the rocks. If she could catch up with Annie, she could grab hold of the tree and stop them from going further downriver. The debris could just as easily trap Annie underwater. Scarlett knew she wasn't strong enough to help either of them if that happened.

Where was J.T.? Had he gone for help? If so, could anyone get to them in time? "Jesus," she prayed again. She didn't know if she said the word aloud or not, but she needed Him more than she ever had.

She reached for Annie just as Annie hit the debris. The little girl went under the water and disappeared. Scarlett slammed into a fallen log she hadn't seen under the surface. For a terrifying moment she thought she would lose consciousness. She kicked at the offending tree and felt something else. Something soft. Annie! She fought through the debris and reached into the water. Her hands closed around a pair of tiny shoulders. She hauled Annie out of the water. Her eyes were closed. Her face was gray and her still lips were blue. If Scarlett had any breath to spare, she would've screamed in shock and fear. All she could do was pull Annie closer.

Annie's eyes popped open. She blinked and took a deep breath. "Mama!"

Scarlett nearly collapsed with relief. Salty tears filled her eyes, hot against the cold water from the stream. She was so weak. She couldn't draw a full breath. She managed to squeeze her legs around a branch to keep them from getting swept away. The branch released beneath the water's surface, and Scarlett was turned in a half circle and jammed against another clutch of debris. Something cracked inside her ribcage. Searing pain shot through her. Annie was wrenched from her grasp and went underwater again. Scarlett tried to scream. She couldn't move. One leg was pinned behind her, while the other was dragged downstream as if the creek was trying to wrench her in half. She inhaled against the pain in her side and stretched toward where Annie had disappeared. Two large hands reached into the water and hauled Annie's dripping body out.

Scarlett couldn't tell who the hands belonged to. All she saw were sodden pantlegs and a pair of boots standing atop the debris before the branches shifted and swept her toward the middle of the creek. Her lungs filled with water. Annie was safe. Nothing else mattered, she thought as swirling water closed over her head.

Chapter Thirteen

Hands closed around Scarlett's shoulders. She winced as branches and debris grabbed and clawed, unwilling to release her to the hands pulling her toward the bank. She thought she recognized Travis's strong hands and powerful chest. It could be her imagination. Travis was mad at her, though she couldn't remember what made her think so.

Another set of hands grabbed her arm. She was dragged to the water's edge and rolled onto the muddy bank. A strong hand pounded her back. She coughed and winced and managed to draw her breath.

"Annie!" she tried to scream. It came out as barely a whisper.

"It's all right. We got her. She's safe."

It *was* Travis. He was here. Past his shoulder, she saw Annie coughing and sobbing against her mother's shoulder while Whit pounded her back. J.T. and Candace stood farther up the bank. J.T.'s face was snow white and his eyes round with fear. Tears streamed down Candace's cheeks.

Scarlett began to shiver, suddenly conscious of the cold and how close she and Annie had come to death. Travis slid out of his coat and draped it over her shoulders. He put his arms around her and helped her to her feet. She looked into his face and burst into hot, wrenching sobs.

❀ ❀ ❀

Scarlett sat in the rocking chair in Carrie and Whit's bedroom, dressed in one of Carrie's warm flannel gowns and a dressing gown. Carrie wanted to wrap strips of cloth around her ribcage in case she'd broken a rib, but it impeded her breathing too much. Marla dressed the cut on Scarlett's calf while all three women discussed how to monitor the rib situation. Scarlett finally convinced them breathing was the immediate need. She'd let them know if she thought her ribcage needed wrapped. She prayed it didn't.

Her wet hair hung loose down her back. Warmth radiated from the chimney on the center wall that rose through the bedroom to the roof. Despite the heat, she couldn't stop shaking. Marla had plied her with hot tea while Carrie soaked her feet in hot water. Still, she shivered.

If J.T. hadn't run for help the instant he saw Annie go into the water…

If their path down the river hadn't been slowed by fallen trees…

If Travis and Whit hadn't been inside the mill and immediately responded to J.T's cries for help…

Scarlett couldn't have gotten Annie out of the water on her own. She and Annie would've been swept downriver for the men of Cowboy Creek to recover later.

She couldn't have saved anyone.

If there'd been any doubt before, she could no longer deny the undeniable. She wasn't fit for life on the frontier. She was a burden, a charity case. She didn't belong here. She couldn't avoid telling Marianne any longer. Though he probably no longer cared, she needed to tell Travis too.

A light tapping sounded on the door lintel. Scarlett took as deep a breath as she could draw and tried to ease the fatigue on her face. Carrie looked in and gave her an encouraging smile.

"How's Annie?"

Carrie advanced into the room. "She's sleeping. She was scared to death at first, but once she realized how much attention she was getting from me and her papa, she got used to it right quick. After a nice hot bath, she went straight to sleep. She might have bad dreams for a while. Maybe the rest of her life. Might be the same for you."

Bad dreams were a small price for Scarlett to pay for her and Annie's rescue. She coughed and tightened the collar of the dressing gown around her. She hadn't experience more severe fits of coughing since the day at the Campbell farm. Even now, her lungs were silent. Maybe they were frozen from the water.

Carrie took a towel from her shoulder and knelt in front of Scarlett. She lifted one foot out of the cooling water. Scarlett tried to pull away. Carrie tightened her grip on Scarlett's ankle. "None of that. There's no shame in accepting help now and then."

Except when you need it all the time, Scarlett thought. But she complied to the woman's ministrations.

"Travis is downstairs," Carrie said gently. "He hasn't left since we brought you and Annie in. He wants to come up."

"What? Oh, no. I can't let him see me like this."

"I'm afraid it won't be that easy." Carrie pushed her feet into a pair of slippers. "I tried to get him to go home an hour ago, but he won't hear of it. He wants to see for himself that you're all right. I think you'll want to talk to him in private. Whit just left to tell Marianne what happened. I'm sure she'll be here in no time."

Scarlett groaned inwardly. Travis *and* Marianne. She didn't want to hurt either of them. She may as well get it over with, starting with Travis. "You can send him up. Or I can go downstairs if that would be more suitable."

"We're not going to worry about propriety today. Marla and I discussed it, and we think it best if you sleep here tonight so I can monitor your ribs."

"Oh, I—"

Carrie silenced her with a firm look. "It's already decided. Marla will stay too. Whit can sleep downstairs on a pallet on the floor with J.T. We girls'll have the upstairs to ourselves."

Scarlett opened her mouth again to protest. Carrie picked up the wash pan and cradled it against her. "You have to let me do this, Scarlett. If it hadn't been for you…"

She sighed tearfully. "I don't know if you know this, but Annie isn't my actual daughter. The poor mite was practically living on the streets in Cincinnati. Her worthless daddy didn't want anything to do with her after her ma died. From the looks of things, he didn't have much to do with her beforehand. Sometimes I wonder if he thinks about her or wonders what became of her. When she's older, I suppose I'll write him a letter and tell him where she is if the neighbors haven't already. That man doesn't deserve a child as precious as Annie."

Her hands clenched around the edges of the wash pan. Scarlett nearly smiled at the indignation on her face.

"I couldn't love her more if she'd come out of my own body." She sniffed away the tears that threatened. "I don't know what I'd've done today if you hadn't been there when she fell into that river."

"I didn't do anything," Scarlett said. "I wasn't strong enough to help her."

Carrie shook her head so hard water splashed onto her blouse. "You did everything. You saved my baby. I'll never forget how you endangered yourself for her." She spun away and hurried out the door.

Scarlett stood and smoothed out the wrinkles in the dressing gown. Outside, rain had begun to fall again, soft and gentle this time. Cleansing. Carrie may never see the truth, but the rest of them would as soon as they heard the whole story. It was only by the grace of God and J.T.'s quick thinking that saved Annie. Not her.

Her heart filled with dread at the sound of Travis's footfalls on the stairs. She folded the blanket that had covered her lap and put it on Carrie and Whit's bed. She should've told Carrie she needed time to dress properly before allowing Travis upstairs. She didn't have any clothes here except for the dress she'd been wearing when she went into the water. Not only would he see her as weak and infirm, but also in a borrowed dressing gown with her wet hair streaming down her back. Could this moment get any more humiliating?

She needed to accept that this was how things were. She wouldn't apologize for it, even if he was about to see her improperly attired. She twisted her hair into a rope, clasped her hands in front of her, and faced the door.

Travis's frame filled the doorway. It was nearly her undoing. He was so handsome. Virile. Strong. Perfectly suited for this life. Her heart ached more than it had a right to that he'd find another woman and take her to live in his house with the walnut door after Scarlett moved to Ruby City.

"I can't thank you enough for what you did for Annie and me—"

He crossed the room in two strides and wrapped his arms around her. "Thank you, God. Thank you. I'm forever grateful." He buried his face in Scarlett's wet hair. She relaxed against his, reveling in his hard chest and strong arms. She thought of his kiss last night and wished he would kiss her again. But that would only make the next few minutes harder.

He pulled away a strand of hair that clung to her cheek. "I should've warned you about the creek after a hard rain. The water comes out of the mountains and rearranges everything. I just didn't realize how dangerous it was today until I saw you and Annie. If you hadn't jumped in after her with no thought for yourself…"

He sounded like Carrie, giving her more credit than she deserved. "It is dangerous. Too dangerous for someone like me. Annie nearly died today. I couldn't do anything for her."

Travis pulled back. "What are you saying? You saved her."

She stepped out of his arms and held the neck of the dressing gown together. "No, I didn't. Anyone else would've pulled her away from the edge before she was swept in. I didn't have the strength. It was my fault she nearly died."

"If you hadn't held onto her as long as you did, she would've been taken downriver. You both would've drowned."

"But I didn't hold onto her. I had her in my hands several times, but she kept slipping away."

"You held her long enough for us to get there. That's all that matters."

"You're not listening, Travis. J.T. is the one who saved her. He ran for help. You should be thanking him."

"Scarlett, stop! Are you mad at me for what happened today?"

"No! Yes!"

She pressed her hands over her eyes. She breathed as deeply as her aching ribs would allow, then lowered her hands. His eyes were dark with confusion. It reminded her of the way he looked last night when he kissed her. "I am mad, Travis," she said evenly, "but only at myself. That child needed saving and I couldn't do it. I knew I couldn't before I went in that water. I wasn't even strong enough to call for help."

She couldn't hold the tears at bay. She allowed him to pull her into his arms. He held her against his broad chest until her tears were spent. Her breath came in short, painful bursts so she didn't have the luxury of crying for long. Later, after her ribs healed, she'd allow herself a long, self-pitying crying fit.

She dried her face with the sleeve of the dressing gown. Before she could say anything, Travis led her to the chair and eased her into it. "I want to apologize for last night."

She looked questioningly at him.

"For kissing you. I'm sorry."

If he was trying to make her feel better, he was doing a poor job of it.

"I'm not sorry I kissed you. I've been wanting to do that for a long time. I'm just sorry for the way I did it. I shouldn't have walked away. I should've told you what was on my mind."

"I sort of wondered…"

He smiled sheepishly. He pulled out the stool under Carrie's dressing table and sat in front of her, their knees only inches apart. "I know you've been keeping something from me. It made me mad. I thought we were both picturing a future together. If that was going to happen, I wanted you to trust me enough to tell me what's going on. To tell me how sick you are. When you didn't even after I brought it up plenty, I thought maybe you didn't think as much of me as I thought of you."

Scarlett's stomach tightened under her sore ribs. The moment of honesty had arrived. She opened her mouth to respond. But what did he just say?

"A future together? We can't have a future together."

"What? Why? I thought that's why you came. We get along well enough. You like me, and I like you. I think it's more than that for me. I thought we'd—"

"Travis, wait. There's something I have to tell you. I'm going to move to Ruby City. I need a job. I need to support myself." The words spilled out over each other.

"What about us?"

"What about us? You haven't proposed marriage. Even if you did, I can't accept. I can't get married."

He raked his hand through his hair. His eyes darkened and his jaw clenched. "Scarlett, you're not—"

She sighed. "Travis, I didn't tell you or Marianne everything Dr. Gaetz said. He advised me to move to the city. Get a job as a schoolmarm or a nanny." She wouldn't mention the doctor's suggestion that she marry a rich man and enjoy a life of ease. "He said I'm not strong enough for life on the frontier. I'd end up working myself into an early grave. After today, I know he's right."

"You don't believe that and neither do I. Your limitations, if that's what you want to call them, mean you might not do every kind of work required out here. You won't go into the fields. If the summer sun gets too hot, you'll sit in the shade and rest. There's plenty you can do. Sewing. Reading to the children."

"No!" She winced against a jolt of pain under her ribcage. "I won't do that. I won't become a burden to you or anyone else. As for children, there may not be any. I may not be strong enough to…" She looked away. She couldn't say the words out loud.

Travis put his finger under her chin and brought her face back to his. "Scarlett, is that what you think of me? I wouldn't want you if you couldn't give me children?"

"I don't want to disappoint you. I don't want you to look back on your life and wish you had chosen someone else."

He shook his head, his eyes simmering. "You wouldn't tell me how sick you were because you figured you knew what was best. Now you won't consider marrying me because you think you know how I'll feel fifty years from now."

"I want you to have a good life."

Travis dropped his head. "So do I. I also should have some say on what that life will look like. My mama treated me the way you are now. She believed she was protecting me by not telling me how sick she was. She still died. The only one she protected was herself against something ugly she didn't want to face."

"That's not what I'm doing."

"I think it is." He looked to the window, though there was nothing to see but rain streaking down the pane. When he looked back, his gaze was dark. Challenging.

"You're not the only one who chooses how much truth to tell. I didn't correct you when you thought I grew up in a hotel. I wasn't. I was born in a brothel. Mama—well, she wasn't a maid. She worked above a saloon. I never knew my pa. Mama was always short on details."

Scarlett could barely draw a breath. Though the confession was simple enough, she couldn't comprehend it.

"There weren't any young'uns in the saloon besides me. Sometimes the girls would find themselves, you know, with a baby coming. Most times, she'd just go away. I was a kid, but I knew better than to ask what became of her. I guess I understood enough to be afraid of the answer.

"One night I heard a baby crying. It was such a foreign sound I asked Mama where it was coming from. She said one of the girls had a baby. I could barely get to sleep. I was so excited to think there'd be another kid for me to play with. The next morning, I didn't hear a baby. Mama said it was too small and didn't live. The real reason, though I didn't know it at the time, was babies were bad for business. Whatever became of it, no one ever said. I remember staring at the girls for the next week, trying to figure out which one the baby belonged to. Of course, I didn't know what to look for. A sad face, maybe. I never figured it out. They all went back to work like nothing happened."

Sadness clouded his eyes. "I never knew why Mr. Keplinger let Mama stay after she got—after I was born. When I was older and understood more of what was going on there, I wondered if he was my pa. Whatever the reason, we stayed. He was always kind to me. Even after Mama got too sick to work, he kept us on. He never did that for other women. Sickness or weariness meant you were out of a job. Customers came to the saloon for a good time, not to think on how the women upstairs were real people with real problems."

He scrubbed his hand over his face. Scarlett wanted to reach out and catch his hand to ease his consternation, but she was too shocked. A brothel? The very thought made her shudder. She had seen the women who worked in those establishments. Watched them stumble along the darkened streets, hanging onto a loud, drunken man. She had wondered how a woman could let herself get into such a state and what type of man would want her. Now Travis was telling her his mother was that very kind of woman.

"I've seen a lot of ugliness, Scarlett," he said as if reading her mind. "Meanness. I saw women with black eyes. Swollen lips. Sprained wrists and dislocated shoulders from getting yanked around. I once saw a gal get shoved down the stairs by a man drunk as a skunk who wanted somebody to kick around. She almost died. She was a real nice girl. Only about sixteen or seventeen.

"There was beauty there, too, believe it or not. Kindness. Most of the women treated me like their own son or a little brother. Looked out for me. Once, I was getting pulverized by a few of the bigger boys in town when two of those gals walked right into the middle of the fight, yanked those boys off me, and took me home. A few of the boys called insults after us, but most of them just watched us go. I wondered at the time why they didn't chase after us and finish what they started. I figure some of their pappies were those gals' regular customers."

He sighed and shook his head as if he couldn't remember why he'd started down this road. "I never told a word of this to anyone. I knew it didn't have anything to do with me. Still, I was ashamed. I know what decent people think of women who work in those places. Of what they think of the men who go there. They're probably right. But circumstances can make a person think they don't have another choice. I don't know. Maybe they don't. I just know I lived through a lot of things that would make respectable society think I wasn't fit to be part of it. That I had no business thinking I could have a life with someone like you. That God could wash the filthiness off me."

Scarlett's heart ached for him. And for herself since she had thought those exact things. "Oh, Travis, I—"

He leaned forward and grabbed her hand. "Scarlett. I think I am deserving of a life with a woman like you. Leastways, I want to try. Life has been hard on both of us. We carry the scars. We can't change anything. We can't clean the muck off on our own. Only God can do that, and I believe He has."

He stood and pulled her up with him. "Do you believe it too, Scarlett? Do you think we can look past the secrets we kept from each other and start something great out here?" He squeezed her hands. "You told me once that hard work was all you ever knew. Life out here won't be easy or without risk to either of us. I'm a little scared of it, same as you. I'm even more scared of imagining it without you."

She wanted to believe him. She wanted to take a chance. But she was afraid. Afraid of letting him down. Of letting Marianne down. Of letting herself down.

"I don't want to be a burden."

"Then don't be. Lean on me and I'll lean on you." He brought her clasped hands to his lips and kissed her knuckles. "I've heard enough wedding vows the last few months. Preach always asks the couple if they vow to love each other in sickness or in health. Before, they were just words. Now I understand. I'm willing to stand before God and everybody in Cowboy Creek and vow to honor and cherish you. To love you no matter what the future brings. Don't walk away from us, Scarlett. Don't let fear of what may happen keep us from enjoying what *does* happen."

"Oh, Travis, you make it sound so simple."

"It can be."

She lifted her arms to put them around his neck and winced against the pain.

He drew back. "What?"

"Nothing. I hurt my ribs when I was in the water."

He put his arms around her and gingerly drew her to him. She was acutely aware of wearing nothing but Carrie's nightdress and dressing gown. She hoped Marianne didn't choose this moment to barge through the door.

He rested his forehead against hers. "There's a big auction barn in Ruby City where farmers sell and trade. Vendors set up stalls and sell baked goods, clothes, knives, guns, horses, all sorts of housewares. Blankets, curtains, braided rugs. Anything a body could want. Maybe we can get hitched on Sunday and go to Ruby City as man and wife. We can buy whatever you like to turn that old cabin of mine into a home."

Scarlett thought she might burst with excitement and hope. "Are you sure? You may get tired of a wife who can't keep up during harvest season."

"And Dr. Gaetz might not know what he's talking about. Didn't you say most of the women improved once they left the factories?"

"I did."

"Then we need to have faith you'll be one of them. If not, we'll deal with it together."

"I'm afraid my faith's not as strong as yours."

"I'm afraid if you don't say yes, I'm going to stand here and kiss you until you change your mind."

She tightened her arms around his neck. "Do you really think your kisses are that powerful?"

"Only one way to find out."

He kissed her cheek, her chin, and her ear before finally finding her mouth. Scarlett relaxed into his arms and prayed he'd never stop.

The End

Nine Brides for Cowboy Creek: Book 8

Rachael

TERESA SLACK

Chapter One

Rachael Zeldin couldn't wait to get home. She gave a little wave to Dora the salesclerk and exited her favorite dry goods store. She worked in one of the finest dress shops in Cincinnati, but she couldn't afford to shop there. That's why she visited the dry goods store on Wilson Avenue not far from her home. In her shopping bag, she carried two simple hats Dora had set aside for her. The straw one had a barely noticeable discoloration on the crown and the velvet one had a bit of raveling on the brim. Rachael was already thinking of how she'd cover the straw hat's discoloration with a flower or ribbon, and how a few deft stitches would repair the raveling on the other. No one but her would know the hats were less than perfect.

In her small apartment, she kept a wide assortment of ribbon, lace, feathers, and accoutrements—also bought at deep discounts in her preferred shops around the city— to turn these simple hats into works of art to rival any sold in Mr. Winegard's shop where she worked.

Last week Mrs. Finnegan at the emporium commented on Rachael's hat and said she'd buy a similar one if Rachael made it for her. Rachael had been over the moon. She'd been designing and creating her own hats and dresses since she was a girl. She had a built a raving, though small, clientele. Mrs. Finnegan's influence could change all that and create more work than Rachael could handle on her own. A few well-received hat designs could lead to gloves, shirtwaists, then entire ensembles.

She suppressed a shiver of excitement. She mustn't get ahead of herself. Her dreams were for someday. Until it happened, she'd work at Mr. Winegard's; learning, growing in her craft, making connections, and dreaming of a little shop that sold clothing to women like her who couldn't afford the prices at his exclusive shop but still desired to look fashionable.

She had been on her own for five years now, and her dream was only a little closer to reality than it had been when Papa passed away. Mama had died two years before him. Her brother ran the lumber mill in the small town where they grew up. Her sister was the schoolmarm and lived with their brother and his wife and looked after their children. That left Rachael on her own. It was just as well. She loved her family, but she found them a little dull and pragmatic. They saw her as an odd duck. They were probably right.

She hadn't been fortunate enough to get married, which was just as well. She had no interest in the smelly, rough-handed men from her hometown. She knew what they were after. They wouldn't take the time to look past her heavy mane of blond hair and heart-shaped face to see the intelligent, creative woman inside with more to offer than scrubbing the softness off her hands on a washboard and rearing a passel of children destined to repeat the depressing cycle.

They must've sensed it since they never expressed an interest in her. With her parents gone and her sister and brother contentedly ensconced in their own lives, she saw no reason to stay where she had no future. Cincinnati beckoned—a city large enough for a woman with her ambition and talent to make something happen.

Landing the job at Mr. Winegard's was a grand step in the direction she wanted to go. After two and a half years, she was still a lowly shop clerk. The clientele had noticed her eye for fashion and often asked her opinion on which hat or dress to purchase for what occasion. While she loved working with beautiful clothes and influencing purchases, she wanted to be recognized by the designers in the back who created the beautiful ensembles for clerks like her to sell out front.

Clerks didn't earn much money, even in upscale shops like Mr. Winegard's. Rachael had spent the last of her savings on the hats and a new stash of supplies. Hopefully her order for Mrs. Finnegan would turn into more and recoup much of it. However, it wasn't money in the bank. She didn't have the luxury of waiting for Mrs. Finnegan's customers to recognize her talent. She needed to eat.

She wouldn't worry about that now. She made a mental checklist of the inventory of supplies in her apartment. She knew just what she'd use to turn the velvet hat into a showpiece. If she couldn't find a buyer for it, she'd wear it herself when she met Edwin for dinner at the end of the week.

Edwin. She nearly swooned at the thought of him.

Edwin Wyden was a retail buyer for Mr. Winegard's shop and other high-end stores around the city. He was dashing and stylish. And so handsome. At thirty, Rachael was well past marrying age—or so she thought until Edwin swept into the shop her first day there and introduced himself. The way he looked at her, singled her out among the other salesclerks, complimented her fashion acumen—it was exhilarating. Edwin made her feel like the most beautiful, witty, charming woman he'd ever seen.

She smiled to herself the way she always did when thinking of Edwin and picked up her pace. Today was Thursday, her half day at work. That gave her all afternoon to work on the velvet hat. Now that she thought about it, she'd just keep it for herself. It would look perfect against her pale blond hair, and the color would bring out her sapphire blue eyes. She couldn't wait to see Edwin's face when he picked her up Saturday. She had only seen him at work once this week. He was always so busy, not that she wasn't herself.

She had never put much stock in love or physical chemistry. The married couples she knew married out of necessity. She doubted love or passion or attraction had anything to do with bringing them together. Until Edwin locked his blue eyes on her. Until he had taken her hand and kissed it and whispered those words in her ear that showed her passion was real, and her life would never be the same without it.

Her jaw tightened as she thought of her coworkers' warnings after her first encounter with Edwin. The chemistry had been so strong even those pinch-faced harpies noticed.

"Be mindful of that one," Beatrice said after Edwin went into Mr. Winegard's office. "He likes the ladies."

"Most men do," Rachael reminded her haughtily. She wasn't a child. She knew the ways of the world.

"Don't believe everything he says either," Justine added. "He's a smooth talker with all the ladies. How do you figure he's moved up so high so fast in his field? He knows just what to say to get what he wants, whether it's a sale..." She looked down her skinny nose. "...or someone like you. He's left a trail of broken hearts all through this city."

Their warnings rankled Rachael. They were jealous that they couldn't attract the attention of someone like Edwin. That's all there was to it.

In the months that followed, Rachael and Edwin's attraction grew. Every time he came in, they found a few moments to talk amidst the hustle and bustle of the shop. They discussed literature, new trends in the clothing line, and Rachael's increasing influence among shop patrons. He was always supportive and encouraging.

She couldn't say anything about her aspirations around the other clerks. She didn't have any close friends with whom to share her dreams. But Edwin cared. He took her seriously. He recognized that she was destined for greater things than working as a lowly clerk forever. He tipped her off to sales in other shops where she could buy odd lots to build up her private stock. With his help she had been able to make hats for women in her neighborhood and at church. She couldn't support herself on the small clientele she served now, but with Edwin's continued support and Mrs. Finnegan's influence, it was a closer possibility than ever.

Someday Mr. Winegard would recognize her abilities and put her in charge of the whole department. When Edwin proposed—yes, she entertained dreams of marriage, especially after last week—they could open a shop together. With her eye for design and his connections and genius for recognizing trends, their business would rival every upscale shop in the city, and remain true to her vision of providing fashion for women like her who weren't born to wealth and privilege.

When Edwin came into Mr. Winegard's and directed that effervescent smile at her, her mind wasn't on business. He made her feel like the only woman in the world. She knew the other clerks were right, and he was a ladies' man. Most salesmen were. The job required a man to become an expert at schmoozing and making each client feel like the only ones who mattered. Rachael understood and appreciated his dedication to his job. Regardless of that dedication, his heart belonged to her.

Her heart swelled as she thought of last Saturday. Oh, Edwin. He was wonderful. Perfect. Everything she never knew she needed from a man.

When he came to the shop on Monday, he was aloof and went straight to the back to meet with Mr. Winegard. Rachael knew what that meant. He didn't want the other clerks to recognize how much they had come to mean to each other. There was only one more logical step. He was going to propose, something he'd never done to another woman. She was sure he was nervous, which only endeared him to her more. She couldn't wait to tell Justine and Beatrice and see the looks on their faces.

With her packages in hand, Rachael hurried across the park to the shopping stalls where she had met a woman who sold beautiful beading and ornamentation for hats at prices she could afford. She envisioned adding some jeweled beading to Mrs. Finnegan's hat to bring out the green in the woman's eyes. Mrs. Finnegan loved showy clothing and the beads would ensure more orders of Rachael's work.

As she stepped onto the sidewalk, she twisted her ankle on a loose brick. She limped to the nearest building and leaned against the wall to resituate her leather boot around her ankle. She silently chastised the city for not taking better care of the streets and herself for not watching where she was going.

When she straightened from picking up her bags, the familiar form of a man in a broadcloth jacket blended into the crowd. Edwin? What was he doing here? He should be downtown at this time of day. He probably knew of the market stalls and was looking for bargains he could pass on to his customers.

Rachael thought of the jewelry store on the next corner. Edwin was headed in that direction. Was that why he was here? He was shopping for a ring, something unique he couldn't find downtown. She didn't want to see him picking out her ring. But, in case she was mistaken, she wanted to make sure it was Edwin. If he turned and saw her, she would smile prettily, put her hand to her bodice, and say, "Why Edwin, darling, whatever are you doing in this neighborhood?"

He would say he had hoped to surprise her. It was a beautiful day. He was buying food at the market for a picnic and then he had a big surprise for her.

How would he propose? Her father was gone. She didn't have a brother or other close male relative of whom to ask permission for her hand. The proposal would be between only them. Her heart ached that her parents weren't here to share her joy. They would be aghast and disappointed over what had happened last week between her and Edwin, not that they ever would've known. Rachael was ashamed for giving into temptation, but she loved Edwin. He was an honorable man. Like her, he wouldn't allow such behavior to happen again until their union had been sanctified by the state.

She would insist they marry at City Hall. She couldn't marry inside the church after they had defiled their union in that way. But she believed God was a God of forgiveness. She had repented with tears and was sure Edwin had done the same. They would never sin so grievously again and would raise their children in the love and admonition of the Lord.

The man in the broadcloth coat slowed to talk to a man operating a booth. Rachael slowed as well. He turned, exposing his profile. She nearly gasped aloud in excitement and delight. It *was* Edwin. The man in the stall wasn't a jeweler, but that was all right. There were lots of interesting stalls in the market square before they reached the jeweler. She and Edwin had strolled around this square many times. She had pointed out things she liked, and he had even bought her a few inexpensive gifts during their forays.

A few weeks ago, she had pointed out a lamp that caught her eye. Was that why he had come here? Not for a ring, but to buy the lamp? Her spirits soared. Their first thing together for their new home. What a thoughtful wedding gift. That was Edwin. Thoughtful and considerate to a fault.

As soon as he proposed, she would suggest they start house hunting. Her tiny apartment wasn't big enough for two—or more. She didn't know where Edwin lived.

When she suggested he show her during one of their outings, he said his neighborhood wasn't suitable for a lady. She was sure he wouldn't want to live there after they married. She had no idea how much money Edwin earned, though he was successful and never seemed short of funds. She couldn't ask. That would be inappropriate, even after they married. Whatever his financial situation, she was fine living in an apartment in the beginning. As long as it was in a nice neighborhood. With a courtyard and a nice church where they could walk to services.

She imagined Edwin pushing a pram with her arm linked through his. She suppressed a sigh. She was getting ahead of herself again. She just couldn't help it.

Edwin started walking again. He hadn't bought anything at the last stall. That was all right. It was impractical to buy items for a house they didn't yet live in. It would be more fun for Rachael to be with him anyway so they could pick out everything together.

She stepped to the side to stay out of field of vision and kept several clusters of shoppers between them as they advanced through the square. When she reached the vendor with the beading accents, she would let Edwin move on without her. He wouldn't be in this part of town unless he was shopping for something special. She wouldn't spoil his surprise, though it took all her resolve not to peck him on the shoulder and smile with delight when he saw her.

Edwin looked in her direction and smiled his enigmatic smile. His throaty, confident laugh drifted over the heads of the crowd. Rachael nearly smiled in return until she realized the smile wasn't directed at her. She hadn't paid any attention to the beautiful auburn-haired woman walking near Edwin until he put his hand on the small of the woman's back and said something in her ear. The woman was elegantly dressed in a forest green dress and jacket that highlighted her hair and olive complexion. She laughed delicately and let her knuckles graze the back of his hand as it dropped from her waist. They stepped apart and continued walking, but their hands and arms bumped together as they smiled affectionately at one another.

Rachael nearly stumbled again though no loose paving stones were the cause this time. Who was this woman? The interaction was too intimate for a sister or acquaintance. She wanted to turn and run. She couldn't risk them seeing her less than twenty feet behind them, but her feet kept propelling her forward through the crowd. As focused as they were on each other, they wouldn't notice her if she was the only other person in the square.

They stopped at a stall stocked with stained glass suncatchers. Rachael stopped at a stall on the opposite side of the causeway and positioned herself so she could watch them without being seen. The beautiful woman leaned close to the suncatchers, her bright eyes wide and perfect rosebud mouth open in delight as she gazed at the displays. She was beautiful. No wonder Edwin couldn't take his eyes off her. Rachael thought of her own secondhand dress, the one she had altered to look new. Next to that woman, she felt shabby and plain. Beatrice and Justine's words came back to mock her.

"Watch out for that one. He likes the ladies."

She wanted to die. Bury her head in shame. She thought of his hands on her the other night with the same intimacy he was now showing the auburn-haired woman. Her face burned. She couldn't tear her gaze away.

Edwin's gaze drifted past the woman. Before Rachael could duck behind something, he spotted her. His eyes widened momentarily. Rachael bit back tears. This couldn't be happening. He recovered from his shock and turned back to the auburn-haired beauty as if Rachael was merely someone he knew from work. Someone unworthy of interrupting his day to acknowledge.

Rachael spun on her heel and hurried out of the market square. Only her shoes and the broken pavement prevented her from running while hot tears coursed down her cheeks.

Though she hated herself for doing so, she cried the rest of the day. She couldn't decide if her tears were over what Edwin had done or from anger directed at herself for having let him do it.

Everything was so clear. The other woman was the reason Rachael could only see him on Saturdays. She was the reason he hadn't shown Rachael where he lived. He hadn't even told her the name of his neighborhood; probably in fear she would show up uninvited.

She was on her bed with her arm over her face when a knock sounded at the door. She knew immediately who it was. Despite her anger and grief, she jumped up and dried her face and straightened her hair and shirtwaist.

She expected contrition and apology. Instead, she saw only irritation and impatience on Edwin's handsome face. He strode in without waiting for an invitation. "Why are you here?" she demanded, though all she wanted was for him to pull her into his arms and beg for forgiveness.

She already knew she would forgive him, no matter what he'd done.

"I never intended to lie to you." It was a statement, not an apology.

Rachael realized what was happening. He didn't care that he had hurt her—he just didn't want her saying anything to the woman or Mr. Winegard and putting him in an uncomfortable position at work.

"She's your wife, isn't she?"

His eyes lit up with genuine mirth. "Oh, Rachael, you know me better than that. I like women too much for something as dull as marriage."

Heat rushed to her face. How could she not have seen it? He wouldn't marry her. He never intended to. Her eyes filled with scalding tears. What had she done? How could she have been so blind? So stupid? She felt sick. She wanted to throw up. It would serve him right if she vomited all over his suede loafers.

"Is that what all women are to you? You take what you want, then move on to the next girl."

He exhaled, the impatience back on his face. "I can't help it if you saw what you wanted to see. I never tried to be anyone other than who I am."

"I thought…you cared for me. I thought we would…" She couldn't say it. He'd already made a big enough fool of her.

He chortled. "You what? You thought I would marry you?" He laughed outright. She wanted to slap him. Claw his eyes out. But part of her still expected him to realize what a huge mistake he was making.

"Dear, dear Rachael." He reached out to touch her cheek, but she jerked away.

"Don't be offended, darling. It isn't you. I have no intention of marrying anyone. I don't plan to ever get tied down. Should I tire of my philandering ways... If the market falls out of imports and I can no longer talk bloated egomaniacs like Mr. Winegard into paying too much for supplies... If I lose my looks and my charm doesn't go as far as it once did, perhaps then I'll choose a wife from one of the city's wealthy families. It certainly won't be a shopgirl well past her prime."

Rachael bit down on her lip to keep from crying out. Edwin went on as if he didn't realize he'd insulted her. "You're a lot of fun, Rachael. Smart. I like smart women. You're also beautiful. You just take yourself too seriously. You took *us* too seriously."

How could he say that after everything they meant to each other? Her head already knew what her heart hadn't accepted. She had been used. "Get out of my house."

He held up his hands. "I'm sorry if you misunderstood my intentions. I know what the other women in the shop said about me. If you had listened to them, we wouldn't have this misunderstanding now."

"Misunderstanding?"

"All I wanted was a little fun. And we did have fun, didn't we? You're not a girl. I thought you were old enough and smart enough to know what a man is looking for when he pays attention to you."

Rachael wanted to scream. Pull his hair out. How dare he even think the things he was saying! Because she wasn't an impressionable girl in the flower of youth, she should be flattered a man like Edwin would give her the time of day?

She wouldn't flatter him further by throwing a tantrum. She'd do that after he'd gone. She went to the door and opened it. "Goodbye, Edwin," she said calmly, her chin held high.

He sighed and moved as if to leave, then stopped. "I trust you won't say or do anything stupid the next time I come into the store."

"Do you mean tell Mr. Winegard who you truly are? Is that why you're here?"

That was all he cared about. He didn't want a spurned lover to ruin his best account. "I'm not going to say anything to anyone," she assured him. How could she? She was already too humiliated for words. It was bad enough she knew what she'd done. She didn't want Justine or Beatrice to find out. If word got to Mr. Winegard, he'd fire her. He wouldn't tolerate a woman of loose morals working in his upscale shop contaminating his respectable clientele, no matter how much the customers loved and admired her.

Rachael spent the weekend in her tiny apartment wondering what to do. How would she face Bernice and Justine and any of the others in the shop on Monday? The moment Edwin breezed through the door, they would see the devastation on her face and know he'd jilted her. She couldn't bear it. She couldn't walk away from her job either. She had worked too hard to get this position. She couldn't go back to the emporium or take a job as a scullery maid or a nanny. Almost more than missing Edwin, she hated to leave Mr. Winegard's with its beautiful clothes and well-dressed ladies who sought out her expertise and flair.

It took all the stamina she could muster to get out of bed Sunday morning and dress for church. After what she'd done, she figured she needed to stop skipping church and get back in the Lord's good graces.

The first person she saw when she walked through the huge double doors was Nan Canfield. Miss Canfield was a regular patron of Mr. Winegard's shop. Rachael had helped her choose the design for an ensemble for a charity gala she was organizing next month. All the women at the shop loved helping Miss Canfield. The commissions were lucrative, and Miss Canfield was pleasant and congenial. Her family had owned several businesses in the city. After her brother died, she became the sole heir to the family fortune—except for a nephew who had moved west if Rachael's memory served her correctly.

She watched Miss Canfield interact with friends and fellow members of several civic organizations. She was virtually alone in the world, yet she had found joy and fulfillment among her church family and social activities and organizations. Rachael could never be that way. First and foremost, she didn't have the means to live in a large house with a household staff and spend her time with church and charitable committees. She would always have to earn a living. On her own.

Miss Canfield caught her eye and broke away from the group. "Good morning, Rachael, dear heart. You look as lovely as ever. That shade of blue is so becoming on you. Have you had a chance to talk with Mrs. Roush about the dresses for her daughter's wedding in the Spring?"

"Thank you for the compliment, Miss Canfield. And no, I haven't. Mr. Winegard told me Mrs. Roush wanted to talk the dresses over with me, but I haven't seen her yet." Her heart tugged. Charlotte Roush's daughter's wedding had been the talk of the shop for the last three months. She wanted Rachael's input on fabrics and designs. One more thing she would miss if she couldn't go back to the shop.

Miss Canfield studied Rachael. "Are you all right? You seem out of sorts."

"Yes. I mean, no. I mean..." Rachael smiled in hopes of disguising her hurt feelings.

"Would you like to come to my house for luncheon today after service," Miss Canfield asked. "We don't know each other very well, and I'd like to rectify that."

"I...I shouldn't. I don't want to be an inconvenience."

Miss Canfield laughed a throaty, comforting laugh that set Rachael at ease. "If it were an inconvenience, I wouldn't have asked. You look like you could use a friend. And perhaps a listening ear."

Rachael nearly burst into tears right then. "I could."

Nan took her elbow and turned her in the aisle. "It's settled then. You can sit with me during service, then after we'll go to my house and get to know each other a little better."

Chapter Two

When he was a boy, Lonnie Fanshaw didn't know he wasn't handsome. He looked just like the man who sat at the head of his dinner table. A bent over man with a nose too small for his face, a forehead too broad, and prematurely thinning brown hair with a cowlick that wouldn't be tamed. None of that seemed to matter to Ma. Her face lit up like a Sunday sunrise every night at the sound of Pa's boots at the door.

When Lonnie first noticed girls, he realized right away they didn't notice him back. A gal wanted a man who cut a fine figure like Adam Waring or a handsome, charismatic fellow like Travis Lindell. Despite his disappointment at being overlooked, he believed he would someday meet the woman who saw past his lantern-jawed exterior and saw the man Ma saw in Pa. Someday he would see the look on that woman's face that he saw on Ma's every time Pa walked into the room. Like she was looking at the handsomest man in town.

Lonnie turned forty-one this past summer—an old man by most accounts. Last Christmas, he had raised his hand along with nearly every other man in Cowboy Creek to express his interest in a bride. His chance at love had probably passed, along with his chance at seeing that look on a woman's face. That didn't stop him from wishing for a bride to share his life. He'd like to hear children playing in his parlor, learning to walk while hanging onto his pant leg, begging for a piggyback ride.

With each bride that came to Cowboy Creek and paired off with someone else, his dream grew dimmer and dimmer. None had given him a second glance. He wasn't surprised in the beginning. Most had come with a cowboy already picked out for her.

Now every man had been claimed but him and Rase Canfield. Rase said he didn't want a bride. Lonnie couldn't understand that. Why would any man choose to live out his days alone with no one to share the most wondrous of God's miracles like a sunrise, the squall of a newborn calf, a prairie twister, a gentle word, a kiss?

The brides had stopped coming. It had been over two months since Marianne and Scarlett Sanders showed up, and they hadn't even been expected.

Last January, Lonnie wrote a letter of introduction like Rase instructed and sent it to Cincinnati along with the others. He wrote that he was a hard worker, he ran a successful business—as successful as one could be in a place as remote as Cowboy Creek. He was fair to middling in intelligence. He could carry on a conversation with most anyone. Politics and theology interested him. He was as well read as a man could be considering his limited access to literature. He even wrote that he wasn't handsome. He hoped that bit of information wouldn't stop a woman of warmth and faith from coming and giving him a chance despite his physical shortcomings.

The year was nearly over. Seven women had come. Seven women had found husbands among the men of Cowboy Creek. Lonnie was the last. Yet he hoped and he prayed. He prayed for patience for himself. He prayed for the woman who would come, that she would be kind and loving and funny and intelligent. And that she wouldn't be disappointed when she laid eyes on him.

Then last month on the day the entire community arrived home after their annual foray to Ruby City to sell their harvest surplus, Marla Dodds came up to him wearing a grin that stretched from ear to ear.

"I believe this is for you, Lonnie," she said as she put a letter in his hand from the post office in Good Hope. She gave him a quick hug before hurrying away.

Lonnie was thrown off by the hug. His first thought was that someone in his family had died. Then he remembered most of them were already gone. The youngest of thirteen children, he had outlived most everybody he knew in the world.

He spotted the postmark from Cincinnati, and his heart nearly stopped.

A woman was coming.

To meet him.

Lonnie read the letter three times before he was satisfied it wasn't a mistake. The woman didn't write much. Her name was Rachael Zeldin. She was thirty years old. He was proud of her for admitting that. Thirty was a kid to him but an embarrassment to most unmarried women. She didn't mention a previous marriage—not that he would've cared. That meant she was probably a spinster. He thought of his spinster schoolmarm back in primary school, Miss Hatchett. Steel gray hair pulled back so tight from her face she could barely close her tiny eyes. Glasses on a chain around her neck and a perpetually pursed mouth that never smiled. She stalked the rows of chairs looking for an excuse to crack a boy's knuckles for the slightest provocation with a long ruler she was never without.

He read the letter for the fourth time and figured even if Miss Hatchett showed up, though she'd be about eighty by now, he'd welcome her into his home with open arms.

Rachael wrote that her parents had passed on. She had a brother and a sister still living in the small town where she grew up, but the relationship didn't sound close. Lonnie got the impression Miss Zeldin wasn't thrilled about coming. She seemed to see Cowboy Creek as her last hope. It probably was for everyone who showed up here. If things had gone well for her in Cincinnati, she wouldn't reach out to a stranger to become his bride.

Whatever had driven her to write to him, she was coming. While he waited, he scrubbed every inch of his house and body. He scrubbed in vain at the black ground into the creases of his hands and under his fingernails. His hands were cracked, calloused, and stained from thirty-odd years of swinging a hammer over a blacksmith's anvil. His shoulders were curved inward, and his face set in a perpetual scowl from squinting against the heat and light from his forge.

He built a rocking chair and set it next to the fireplace. He imagined a woman—Rachael, maybe—sitting in that chair with a baby. If it didn't work out between them, he could use the chair for himself. Lonely old men were as partial to rocking chairs as nursing mothers, he reckoned, should he end up alone.

Though no one would know by his calm exterior, his heart rattled a rapid drumbeat inside his chest while he waited in the early November thaw for the stage to roll up. He heard the rattle of the old stage a long minute before it rolled into view between the dilapidated buildings. Good Hope could've done him a favor and made a better first impression by letting the sun appear from behind a heavy sky of gray clouds. It would've been nice if the bitter wind pulling at Lonnie's hat and coattail stopped blowing for a minute or two. Neither of those things happened. Grimy patches of snow littered the ground from the first measurable snowfall last week. It was cold. The kind of wet cold that settled into a man's bones and stayed there.

Lonnie stamped his feet to temper his impatience and keep his blood flowing. He'd been standing here for twenty minutes. He could've waited in the café, but everyone in Good Hope knew about the line of women who had passed through here to get to Cowboy Creek. Every loafer and farmer in the café would know what he was doing in town on a Monday. He wasn't bothered by a good-natured ribbing. He did plenty of ribbing himself. But he wouldn't get teased like the other men who'd taken brides. Oh, no. Lonnie would get pity. Poor old, delusional Lonnie Fanshaw waiting on a woman. Didn't he know no woman worth having would want to move to the middle of nowhere with an old man as homely as him and live in his blacksmith shanty.

Lonnie already had enough of those doubts himself. He didn't need to see them on the face of every farmer in Good Hope. When the stage pulled to a stop, he forgot about the cold seeping through his boots and what the people watching from the warmth of the café across the street might be saying and speculating.

"Afternoon, Lonnie. Waitin' long?" The driver Ace Bradley called down to him.

"Naw," Lonnie lied. "Have a nice ride?"

"Roads're a fright. The ruts are frozen just enough to purt near rattle a man's teeth outta 'is head." Ace set the brake and tightened a tattered scarf around his neck, tucking twelve inches of matted gray beard inside. "Cold enough too. My passenger's probably froze solid inside that coach. I 'spect she's here for you."

Lonnie gulped, suddenly a bundle of nerves. He smoothed a hand down over his wool coat, the one that only came out of the closet on Sunday mornings. Should he wait for Ace to disembark or open the door himself? He didn't want to look like a coward, but he sort of was. He imagined her taking one look at his haggard face and slamming the stage door shut.

"Take me back to Denver!" he almost heard her shout to Ace.

He was being ridiculous. This was the moment he'd been waiting for since last Christmas. He took a deep breath and pulled out the hinged step that made disembarking easier for lady travelers, then opened the door. The loveliest creature he'd ever laid eyes on placed a delicate hand in his gloved paw. The bitter cold had done Lonnie one favor. The first thing Miss Zeldin saw of him would not be his stained, cracked hands.

Her hand rested in his as light and delicate as a bird. They were gloved in black leather with tiny black pearl buttons all the way past her wrist. She was bundled against the weather in a long velvet, fur-lined cape of forest green. The hood of the cape was up, covering most of her face. She wore a hat under the hood so he couldn't tell what color her hair was. It didn't matter. He'd find her beautiful if she had no hair at all.

Two dainty black boots stepped into the muck beside him. The moment of truth had arrived. He hoped she couldn't tell through their gloved hands that his were shaking. He took another deep breath to ease his nervousness and smiled. He hoped the smile looked warm and friendly and not like a grimace. He'd lost a canine tooth a few years ago, and it hadn't done his appearance any favors.

He tried not to brace himself for the look of distaste that would surely appear when she saw him up close. He'd seen it a million times. The look that quickly skittered past him looking for a more attractive prospect on which to land.

To be fair to Miss Zeldin, the brief flash that passed through her amethyst eyes was so quick Lonnie would've missed it if he wasn't looking for it. She didn't look away. Her gaze stayed. On Lonnie. And she smiled.

Lonnie felt that smile all the way down to his nearly frozen toes.

"Miss Zeldin?"

She swallowed, the movement disappearing down her pale white throat into the fur-lined cape. Lonnie tried not to gape. She spoke in a voice as smooth as honey. "Mr. Fanshaw?"

"I sure am." Did he sound too eager? What did he care? He was eager.

"I'm pleased to meet you, Mr. Fanshaw."

She looked like she really meant it. "I'm most pleased to meet you, ma'am. It's been a long time."

There he went sounding overeager again. She didn't need him to point out his age or the fact that women had given him a wide berth his entire life.

She shivered inside her cape. "Yes, thank you. I didn't expect it to be so cold this early in the season."

Lonnie snapped to attention. "Oh, yeah. I'm sorry." As if the weather were his fault. "I'll get your things. Isn't always this cold. Cold spell should break in a day or two. They usually do when they hit this early."

The end of a rope dropped off the top of the stage and smacked the side of the coach next to Lonnie, cutting off his diatribe on the weather. He and Rachael looked up at Ace unlashing the last of the cargo. He tossed a mailbag down to Lonnie, along with a canvas sack that rattled against his hands, indicating it was headed to the trading post in Cowboy Creek.

"You don't mind delivering this to Preach, do ya, Lonnie?" Ace asked as he climbed off the stage. "Miss Zeldin's things are in the back."

The three of them went around the stage to the boot where two trunks and two carpet bags had been lashed. Miss Zeldin reached for one, but Lonnie and Ace stepped forward and made quick work of unloading everything. They stacked the bags on top of the trunks and expertly loaded it all into the back of Lonnie's rig. He was glad he hadn't driven the cumbersome buckboard. The carriage was more comfortable and would get them home and out of the cold much quicker.

Ace tipped his hat and headed back to the stage, which he would stow in the stables for the night. Lonnie turned back to Rachael. Without anything more to do but head home, they needed to get on their way.

Chapter Three

Rachael hoped Lonnie hadn't noticed her reaction. She abhorred rudeness, especially in herself. He had described himself in the letter he sent, so she hadn't expected a prince. Still, she had been momentarily surprised. She hadn't expected him to be so…old. Forty-one was just a number until she saw the lines on his face, the gray that threaded his thinning hair, and his stooped shoulders.

Her mother would've called him hatchet-faced, all angles and sharp planes. "My knight in shining armor," she thought to herself.

His smile, though a little off-center, was warm and friendly as were his brown eyes. Rachael felt drawn to them.

She hadn't written much in the letter she sent to Lonnie. What was there to tell besides she had incredibly bad judgment in men? She had humiliated herself and could never show her face in front of her coworkers or friends at church. That's why she was here. No other reason.

Looks didn't matter, she told herself. All that mattered was the here and now, and Lonnie Fanshaw had good manners and he could provide for her. She wasn't exactly a work of art herself. Edwin had proven that by throwing her aside as soon as he got what he wanted. She wouldn't compare this man to Edwin. Edwin was charming and as smooth as a duck's back. She learned too late that charm masked a snake. She could easily forfeit a handsome face if she could have a kind nature and an honest tongue in its place.

The stage driver walked away, leaving her and Lonnie in the middle of the deserted street. "Would you like something to eat? Or a hot drink before we get started?" He nodded his head in the direction of a few buildings across a rut-pocked street.

The few buildings were faded and bleached from the sun and wind. Most didn't have signs identifying their purpose. The street was no more than an open space, dotted with horse dung and potholes big enough to swallow a person if she wasn't paying attention to where she stepped.

"You mean we aren't there yet? This isn't Cowboy Creek?"

Amusement flashed across those brown eyes. "No, ma'am. This is Good Hope. Cowboy Creek is down the road a piece. Good Hope is as far as the stage comes. I'd'a thought Ace explained that to you."

"Oh. Well, um, maybe he did. I'm rather tired." She shivered again and pulled her cape tighter around her shoulders. She had nearly left the cape behind with the things she donated to the church. It seemed too fancy for life on the prairie, but it was also warm and her favorite garment. Now she was glad she brought it. If this dreary settlement wasn't Cowboy Creek, it would be a long time before she could replace it.

She glanced at the gray sky. The sun hadn't made an appearance in three days. She couldn't tell exactly what time it was, but it had to be late in the afternoon. Her stomach rumbled, though she was half sick from bouncing around in the stage. She doubted she would be able to eat a bite.

"How much farther is it?"

"About five miles. We'll be there in an hour, so long as the roads cooperate," he added with a smile she was beginning to like.

She groaned inwardly. Another hour on these rutted, winding, cow paths they called roads. She swallowed hard and managed to smile. "If you don't mind, unless you have errands to run, I'd rather we finish the journey."

Lonnie looked toward the skies. He hunched his shoulders and blew out a puff of air, visible in the space between them. "I was sorta hoping you'd say that. I don't know about you, but a warm fire and hot cup of coffee never sounded better."

She smiled genuinely. "I couldn't agree more."

They went around the side of the carriage. Lonnie took a folded buffalo blanket off the seat and draped it over his arm. He assisted her into the carriage and then settled the blanket over her lap. The heavy warmth was delicious. Rachael sighed in contentment, the tension, sore muscles, and knotted stomach of the last few days momentarily relieved. "Thank you, Mr. Fanshaw."

"Lonnie."

Rachael nodded. "Yes. Lonnie." If she was going to stay here, she might as well get used to his name.

Of course she would stay. What choice did she have? She couldn't show her face in Cincinnati after making such a public fool of herself over a cad like Edwin.

A few long strides, and Lonnie had settled into the seat beside her and set the carriage in motion.

With each of the wheel's rotations, Rachael's stomach churned. Inside the stage, she had eaten her last small, shriveled apple and a dry biscuit she saved from dinner last night at the hotel. Now she wished she hadn't. The apple sat like a rock on her stomach. Her back ached and a headache had formed at the back of her skull.

She gazed around the landscape. Stands of trees crowded along the road, bare and bleak. She could see for miles, and what she saw wasn't awe-inspiring. Nothing but lonely, stark landscape. No sign of life but narrow wheel ruts grooved into the soil stretching ahead as far as she could see. The empty landscape was unnerving. She grew up in a small town outside of Cincinnati, but even that had always shown signs of life. She knew every inch of it. Every worn path to a friendly neighbor's door. Every chimney with smoke curling out the top into a gray winter sky. The snap of clothes on a line. The tangy smell of blacksmith smoke. The clang of a spoon against a pot. A cow lowing or a dog barking. Even though her town was small and isolated, there had always been something going on to remind her she wasn't alone.

Out here the quiet and isolation pressed in on her like a weight.

"It's only five miles," she said to herself. "That's nothing compared to how far you've come."

"Excuse me?"

She snapped her head around to look at Lonnie. She hadn't realized she'd spoken aloud. "I'm sorry. Thinking out loud, I suppose."

He grunted. "No harm in that. Been known to do it myself."

She managed a weak smile. What had she done? According to his letter and Nan's description, Cowboy Creek was a small settlement occupied by hardworking Christian men who wanted to carve a life out of the hostile surroundings. Was she up to it? If her queasy stomach was any indication, she wasn't.

"Did you have a nice trip?" he asked.

"It was long," she said truthfully. And exhausting and noisy and smelly. She appeared to be the only person onboard the train who had thought to pack a bar of soap. She kept that part to herself. "I've never traveled on a train before. I fear the motion was…rather unsettling."

He looked disappointed. She could tell he wanted to start a conversation. She just wasn't up to it.

"I've never been on a train myself." He pushed his hat back on his head. The hat had mashed down his mousy brown hair, revealing a rapidly thinning pate. Oh, dear, he'd be completely bald in another five years.

Apparently, he was determined to fill the ride with conversation. "I came to Cowboy Creek from Michigan with some traveling companions after my folks died. We heard tell there was gold out west. Didn't have anything to prevent us from coming and see if we could find our share. So here we are." He threw up his hands. "Or me anyway. I'm still here. The three of us pooled our money and bought a claim. Didn't take long to figure out there was more money shoeing horses, sharpening shovels, and filling the needs of the miners than hunkering down on a riverbank praying to find a chunk of gold. My pappy ran a foundry back home. Taught me everything I know, so I just fell back into what I'd always done."

He sounded like a smart businessman. But she wondered why he was so keen on staying in a place like Cowboy Creek working for a handful of settlers. How much money could be made off them?

"Did you ever think about going back to Michigan? Don't you miss home?"

He thought about it for a moment. "It wasn't really home after my folks died. I had a handful of brothers and sisters. I was the baby. By the time I came along Mama and Pappy were getting up in years, so I ended up staying with them after they got too old to take care of themselves. When they died, well, everyone else in the family had done moved on. I thought I might like to see a little of the world myself. Weren't nothing tying me down, so I lit out."

Rachael stiffened beside him. *Nothing tying him down.* Edwin had said the same thing. He wanted the freedom to do whatever he wanted with whomever he wanted. She glanced at Lonnie from around the brim of her hood. He seemed nothing like Edwin, but maybe all men were the same to some degree. She hitched the edge of the buffalo blanket up a little on her arms. If her back wasn't so sore, she could nearly snuggle inside it and go to sleep.

"Once I saw this place, I didn't want to go anywhere else." Lonnie straightened in the seat and gazed around, his eyes wide with wonder and delight. "This here's about the prettiest place I ever saw."

Rachael followed his gaze and strained to see what he was looking at. There was nothing pretty about it as far as she could see. Just bleak and cold and stark. Maybe in the spring when the hills came alive with color. But not now. Not today.

Lonnie didn't seem to notice her lack of enthusiasm. "The people are kind too. Hard working. Generous. My friends were anxious to move on once the gold played out. They had caught the gold fever by that time and were sure they'd strike it rich if they kept digging. We heard of a place called Alaska. You know where that is?"

She nodded, though she had only heard the word in passing and didn't know anything about it. "Vaguely."

"They say the rivers are full of gold up there. Everywhere you look. I reckon a man could make a nice living off the folks needing shovels and picks and sled runners." He chuckled. "Michigan's cold enough for me. They say the snow never melts in Alaska and it's so close to the North Pole, the sun never sets." He shook his head. "Can you imagine?"

She couldn't. It sounded horrible.

"I reckon it'd be something to see," he said. "After a quick gander, I'd be ready to turn around and run back home. Don't get me wrong. It gets cold here too, and the snow can really pile up, but nothing a body can't get used to."

Rachael smiled appreciatively. He had a unique way of looking at things. And a unique way of expressing himself. But she still couldn't see much of interest around her. Maybe Cowboy Creek was more picturesque and would explain his fascination with the area.

He kept his bright eyes on her as he talked. His face was animated, exposing a gap where he'd lost a tooth. Edwin had white, straight teeth and an equally animated expression when telling a story. It was what had first attracted Rachael to him. He was also intelligent and well read and could hold a group in the palm of his hand. But that was about where the resemblance ended. Edwin's hair was ebony black, and he wore it slicked back with a pomade that kept every hair in place. Lonnie's looked like it had been combed once today, but taking his hat on and off had mashed one side, and a stubborn lock fell over his forehead. The cut along the back of his neck was a little crooked. Rachael wondered if he cut it himself. She supposed that was a wife's job. Her job, possibly. The thought filled her with sadness. She'd never seen Edwin with a stain on his suitcoat, a frayed cuff, or loose button. Lonnie's coat was clean and stiff from little use, but it was terribly out of fashion and made from low-quality fabric.

A cool wind skittered through a gap in the hills. It rustled the fur on the cape around her face and stung her cheeks with unshed snow. She hoped they got to Cowboy Creek before it snowed again. She couldn't remember seeing snow this early in the season back home. She huddled deeper under the buffalo blanket. She was thankful he'd thought to bring it. She wondered if he was thoughtful in other ways as well, unlike Edwin who seldom asked what she was thinking or what she wanted to do. He was fun to be around but terribly narcissistic now that she thought about it.

"What about you?" Lonnie asked.

She looked at him blankly. His last words were about Alaska. Was he asking if she'd ever been there or ever wanted to? She was just too cold and miserable to follow a conversation.

"Have you ever heard of or read about a place you'd like to see?" he clarified.

"No.." she began, then a memory sparked in her mind. "When I was a girl, I read a book about a young woman in London. The book described London Bridge, the River Thames, the Tower of London. It sounded like a magical place. Full of beautiful, historic places and interesting things. I mean, can you imagine living in a city where you walk past a castle every day on your way to the market?"

"No, I can't say that I can. Don't reckon I know much about London 'cept that's where Shakespeare hailed from."

She nearly fell out of the carriage. "You know Shakespeare?"

He chuckled at the expression on her face. "We had to read some of his writings in school. I never could understand much of what he was trying to say. The language sure was hard to wrap my mouth around. My friends hated it and groaned and moaned every time the teacher opened the book. I sort of liked it myself. I knew ole Will was trying to tell us something and it would take a little studying to figure it out. Sorta like the Bible. I didn't want to look like a teacher's pet by asking questions or paying much mind to the reading. But I would've liked to study his writing more. Then some years ago I found a used book in a little store somewhere. I bought it and stuck it in my saddlebag right quick so no one would see."

He laughed at himself. "I was a grown man by then and still afraid of what my friends would think if they caught me struggling over the words of a long-dead fancy pants English writer."

Rachael smiled back. She couldn't imagine Edwin reading Shakespeare or admitting something that made him look silly. There was more to this plain-faced cowboy in the middle of nowhere than she would've dreamed. He wasn't handsome, but he was interesting and funny. He didn't fit her image of a knight in shining armor, but she might just like to get to know him better.

The wagon hit a rut in the road and threw her against him. Rachael threw her hand out to steady herself. It landed on Lonnie's leg. She jerked back, aghast. "I'm...I'm so sorry." Her face flamed.

Lonnie didn't appear to have noticed. "We travel this road a lot back and forth to Good Hope. Maybe in the spring, I'll see about getting some of the men to help dig out the worst of the ruts and clear back the trees to make it wider. That'd make traveling easier on you ladies."

He was assuming a lot, Rachael thought. She hadn't said she'd be here in the spring. He hadn't even asked. Of course, she was here. Why else would she have come if she didn't plan to stay? Her stomach rolled again with another pitch of the wagon. She hoped she hadn't just made the biggest mistake of her life. An even bigger mistake than Edwin.

Chapter Four

The wagon rolled to a stop in front of a gray weathered building that looked like the first stout wind would blow it over. A small porch was built on the front and covered by a tilted roof. A large barn separated it from a tiny house that showed signs of habitation. The roof had been patched multiple times. One of the windows was boarded over and the front door didn't fit tightly against the peeling door jam. Across the worn path were scattered a few other buildings, looking equally forlorn and forgotten.

Rachael sat up straight and looked around. She became aware her jaw had gone slack. She jerked her mouth shut and turned incredulous to Lonnie. "Is this…it?"

Lonnie smiled proprietarily. "Welcome to Cowboy Creek."

"But…" Rachael didn't want to insult him since he was apparently so enamored with the place. "It's—where are the people?"

He kept smiling. "Oh, they're around. Up that way is my place. Through the trees you can see my shop. It's easier to see in the daylight. My living quarters are attached to the back. I know it doesn't sound like much, but it's not bad. Convenient for me too. I'd be most pleased to show it to you someday. On past it in the bend of the creek is the mill. The Whitamores live there; Whit and Carrie and their three young'uns."

Tears pressed at the back of Rachael's eyes. She knew from his letter that Cowboy Creek was remote. But when she read that he lived in town, she thought...well, she thought it was a *town*. Not a handful of shacks scattered along a bend in a river.

What had she done? How would she live here?

She fought down the urge to throw up. Or burst into tears. She couldn't decide which she wanted to do more.

Lonnie threw aside the corner of the buffalo robe that was covering his legs and hopped out of the wagon. Rachael didn't look down at him. She knew he was looking at her for a reaction. He wanted her to be as pleased with this place as he was. She had never been good at hiding her feelings. He would see her dismay all over her face.

The front door of the little business burst open and a woman stepped out. "I thought I heard you," she told Lonnie. "Daniel, they're here," she called over her shoulder. She clasped a crocheted shawl around her shoulders and stepped off the porch. "I was hoping you'd get here before it started snowing again." She looked past Lonnie to Rachael, still frozen in place in the seat. "We're fixing to get more snow. Hopefully not much. It's still early for snow. Daniel, are you coming? They're here," she called again without taking her eyes off Rachael.

She closed one fist around the shawl and reached for Rachael with the other. "You're a sight for sore eyes, darlin'. I reckon you're happy this trip's over. I'm Marla Dodds. Daniel!"

"I'm right here." A smiling older gentleman stepped out the door. He reached the wagon in three surprisingly long strides considering his age.

Rachael took Marla's hand and stood. The man she called Daniel quickly stepped forward and took her elbow to assist her down while Lonnie went around the wagon to unload her things.

"I'm Daniel Dodds," the man said with the warmest, kindest smile Rachael had seen in a long time. "And this is my wife Marla. We own the trading post. Everyone around here considers me the town minister, though I never had any formal training. Everybody calls me Preach 'cept for Marla. Right over there is our community meetinghouse. We have Sunday services there every week. We'd be most pleased to have you join us."

"Well, of course, she'll join us," Marla said. She adjusted Rachael's velvet cloak around her shoulders. "My goodness it's cold. We can talk about all this inside. Lonnie, you and Daniel take Miss Zeldin's things into the brides' house. I've already got the fire laid out. All you gotta do is light it and it'll be nice and warm for her after we eat."

"Oh." Rachael looked around. "I have my own quarters?"

Marla straightened her shoulders. "You certainly do. That little house right on the other side of the barn. It's been occupied by seven brides before you. It's small but warm and cozy. Well, mostly warm. Anyway, that's where the brides stay until…well, until you decide if you're compatible and desiring to stay."

Rachael looked toward the little house. "If it's all right, if you don't mind, I'd prefer to go there now and settle in. It's been a long journey and I'm awfully tired."

Marla's broad smile settled into the folds of her face. "Oh. Well, I suppose, but what we typically do is have a nice supper waiting for you. That way you can eat a hot meal while we get to know each other. And you can get to know Lonnie a little better—"

Preach set his hand on Marla's shoulder as he looked at Rachael. "We understand perfectly. It's been a trying journey, I'm sure. Marla can walk you over while Lonnie and I unload your things and light the fire for you. We can bring you something to eat if you like after you settle in."

It was obvious she had hurt Marla's feelings, but Rachael was too worn out to feel overly bad about it. There'd be plenty of time to get to know everyone later.

"A little warm broth would be heavenly, and maybe a piece of bread, if it's not too much trouble."

Marla's eyes filled with concern. "Broth? You're not sick, are you?"

"No, no. Just tired. The motion from the stage and the strange foods—I need a little time to let my stomach settle."

Marla seemed to understand she didn't want to discuss the motion sickness in front of the men. "Well, if you're sure…"

"We'll give you all the time you need." Preach took her small carpetbag out of her hands and tucked it under his arm. He offered an elbow to Rachael and took Marla's hand in his and walked the women across the small space.

In the short time it took the men to get the fire going and bring in Rachael's trunks and bags, Marla had showed her around the small house. It only consisted of two rooms—a living and kitchen area and a tiny bedroom no bigger than a closet. But Marla was right. It was tight and cozy and the fire in the pot-bellied stove warmed it up nicely in minutes. Cheery curtains covered the window. A bright coverlet lay on the bed and several rag rugs warmed the floors. It had been swept clean. Rachael couldn't see much outside, but she could tell the windows had been freshly washed.

"This is lovely," she told Marla, regretting her earlier harsh judgment of the place even if no one knew of it but her.

"Each bride before you has put her personal touch on the place. I'm sure you will too." The older woman pointed to a trunk on the floor. "You might find some odds and ends of fabric and clothing in there. Feel free to use whatever you like. Make it your own."

Rachael unbuttoned her cloak and slipped it off her shoulders. "I'll do that. Thank you very much."

Marla grinned. "Don't thank me. Thank the women before us. I'm afraid there might not be much left. But help yourself to anything that'll make you more comfortable."

Rachael glanced around the room for a hook on the wall. All she saw was a row of nails. She wouldn't risk her beautiful cloak by hanging it on a nail. She laid it out gently on the narrow bed behind the stove. It was wrinkled and dulled with soot and dust from the trip. First thing tomorrow, she would knock off as much of the dust as she could and straighten out the wrinkles.

She turned and saw Lonnie watching her. Her face colored. He looked away as if embarrassed to watch her do something so intimate. The tiny room's walls seemed to close in even tighter. She took a deep breath. She wished they would hurry up and leave. She wanted to lie down. Her headache had intensified now that the cabin was warming up, and the extra people in it seemed to trip over each other.

Preach slammed the wardrobe doors after setting her carpetbags inside. "Well, that should do you. There's plenty of room to hang your things. There's enough wood here to last through the night. Plenty more stacked alongside the barn. Take whatever you need." He put his hand on the small of Marla's back to turn her toward the door.

"I'll bring that broth right over," Marla said "Or if you change your mind, you're welcome to come over for a proper supper. I…we look forward to getting to know you."

"Come along, Mother." Preach gave his wife a little push toward the door. "Plenty of time for that."

Lonnie hadn't spoken while he and Preach worked. Gone was his earlier animated self. Now, he nodded at her and mumbled a half-hearted *Ma'am* as he went out the door behind Preach and Marla. Guilt pricked at Rachael. He had been nothing but kind and helpful, and she had gone and disappointed everyone by turning down Marla's invitation to supper. The woman had probably cooked and prepared all day. Rachael would make it up to everyone tomorrow. For now, she needed time to put her feet up and take a breath. To get her bearings. And hopefully settle her stomach and headache with a little broth.

She wrapped her arms around herself despite the warmth, which was getting quite stuffy, and turned in a slow circle. She thought of the seven women who had stayed her before her and wondered if they had felt as overwhelmed and anxious as she did now.

"Lord, what am I doing here?" she asked aloud. "Is this what you want for me? Or have I piled another mistake on the ones I already made?"

She looked at the door where Lonnie had just exited. He seemed like a nice man. Thoughtful. Hard working. The type who would look after a wife. Provide for her. Give her a comfortable life—as comfortable as one could have in a place like this. Was that enough? She missed the city. She missed the people. The bright clothes and swishing skirts. The bustling streets. The patrons who came into the shop and asked specifically for her before spending their money. She always felt important then. She was nothing here. Just another frontier bride who would wear herself and be buried on the hillside and no one would remember anything about her.

Was it too much to ask for a spark in the pit of her stomach when she thought of her future husband? She couldn't imagine experiencing a spark or anything else over the stoop-shouldered man with the huge hands and high forehead who just walked out the door.

She was still staring at the door, second guessing every decision she ever made when Marla came back with the broth.

Chapter Five

Rachael slept later than usual the next morning. Her appetite was back, which was a good sign. She quickly prepared for the day and hurried across the yard to the door at the back of the trading post Marla had pointed out to her last night. Marla said the brides usually took their meals with the Doddses. Rachael had probably missed breakfast. She hoped there was some porridge or biscuits and honey left over. After a day and a half of eating practically nothing, she was famished.

Marla answered her knock with a wide smile. She didn't look the least out of sorts at Rachael for turning down the supper invitation last night.

"No need to knock, especially when it's this cold," she said. She shivered dramatically and pulled Rachael to the table. "We might be in for a long, cold winter. They're all cold and long around here. Have been for as far back as I can remember."

Rachael basked in the warmth of the stove. She hadn't had much luck getting the stove going in the brides' house this morning, even though the coals still glowed hot. Something was probably clogging the flue. If she couldn't figure it out, she'd need to ask for help. It sounded like a blacksmith's job.

Marla guided her to a chair. "Daniel and I ate an hour ago. I figured you'd sleep in, so I left you some bacon and scrambled eggs. I hope that's all right."

"It sounds heavenly. I feel much better this morning."

"Well, you look better. Got a little color in your cheeks. Did you sleep well?"

"Yes, thank you. All I needed was a solid surface under me instead of the rocking of the stage or the train. Please, you don't need to serve me," Rachael said as Marla set a plate and fork in front of her.

"I don't mind. It's just for this morning since it's your first day, and you had such a trying journey. Now that harvest is over, I have a lot more time on my hands. We'll spend the next few months catching up on chores that have waited all year. We women talked about holding a quilting bee if the weather cooperates.

"In Ruby City there's a market where people sell all sorts of baked goods and household wares. Katie Jamison knows how to make baskets. She said if we can round up the supplies, she'll teach the rest of us, and we can rent a stall next year to sell them. I think it would be such fun. You'll notice soon enough, most of our brides are…" She glanced toward the door to make sure they were still alone. "…With child," she whispered. "Our first little one might make an appearance before the end of the year." Marla beamed like a proud grandmother. "I don't know how much free time you ladies will have then for baskets or anything else."

Rachael thought it a little presumptuous to include her with the other women. She'd just met Lonnie yesterday. She certainly hadn't given any thought to children. She might as well get used to it, though. She had committed herself the moment she climbed aboard the train in Cincinnati.

Marla clasped her hands again and her eyes gleamed. "We already have a few children in Cowboy Creek, and oh, I'm looking forward to more. If you don't mind helping—if you feel up to it, that is—I could use some help cleaning and sorting items in the trading post."

Rachael slathered butter on a piece of toast. "I don't mind at all." The last thing she wanted was to sit in the little brides' house all day and think about the worm Edwin, even though a large part of her still missed him.

After she ate, she insisted on washing her dishes and cleaning the stove. Marla kept up a steady stream of conversation. Rachael talked mostly about her childhood and deftly steered the conversation away from her decision to come to Cowboy Creek. She didn't want anyone to know she had been jilted. It was bad enough Justine and Beatrice, and even Mr. Winegard, had probably figured out by now that her hasty departure was related to the suave Mr. Wyden they warned her against.

After the kitchen was restored to rights, she followed Marla through the living quarters to the trading post. Preach was moving a standing rack of shelves away from a wall in the back. "I thought we'd clear out this section to make room for hardware and ammunition. It'll be out of your way, and you can have the front of the store for items for the ladies."

"I was thinking the same thing," Marla exclaimed. "I'd like to put the fabrics and housewares in front of the window. It's so dark in here, the ladies can barely see what they're looking at."

"Have you considered adding another window," Rachael asked.

Marla and Preach stared at her. Rachael pointed to the only existing window near the front door. "The light through there is blocked by the porch roof. If you moved those barrels and put a window on the east-facing wall, you'd have light most of the day."

Preach scratched his chin. "I never thought of adding another window."

Marla sniffed. "Neither have I."

Rachael went to the wall and stretched her hands as far apart as they would reach. "Right here is perfect. You could make a display window, a big one. Perhaps drape some fabric over a dress form so the women can picture the clothes they could make. If you have extra of a material you hope to get rid of, you could display it in the window and sell more of it that way. Hats would be a nice addition. If you have an extra bureau, you could put it next to the dress form. You could store gloves and handkerchiefs in the bureau and let them spill out of the partially opened drawers. It's an attractive display and makes for good storage for overstock."

"Oh, my, you must've worked in sales," Marla said. "Our little trading post will rival the stores in Good Hope."

Preach pulled on his whiskers. "I don't know about that, but the extra light sure would make doing paperwork easier on my old eyes."

Marla beamed at Rachael. "Honey, you're a godsend. The next warm day we'll cut a window in that wall. If we don't have enough glass, we can pick up a sheet the next time we're in Good Hope. By Spring we'll have a huge display window. Between the two of us we'll talk Daniel into putting one on the opposite wall. It'll be beautiful in here. I'd appreciate any other expertise you have. We've been catering to men for so long who don't care about anything but buckets and shovel handles, we forgot how to run a real store."

Rachael barely noticed the praise. The trading post's dingy interior needed a lot more help than a window, but she wouldn't overwhelm her hosts too quickly. She had plenty of practical ideas to make the place more functional for its owners and shoppers alike, but she'd save them for later. A new window was enough of an improvement for now.

Lonnie hammered the last metal hook into shape and held it up in the light with his tongs. Satisfied it was the same height and length as the other three he'd made, he set it on the anvil and rummaged through a barrel of scrap wood until he found a suitable piece. Working on a project usually took his mind off bothersome topics. Not today.

He wasn't sure what to think of Rachael Zeldin. She sure was pretty—beautiful even. Too beautiful for him and maybe too beautiful for Cowboy Creek. But that wasn't what concerned him. She was quiet. Somber. He had tried to get her talking on their way home from Good Hope, but she hadn't said more than a few words at a time. The only topic that piqued her interest was London. And she sure wasn't going to find anything that rivaled London around here. When he tried to explain why he loved Cowboy Creek so much, she'd looked at him like he had horns on his head.

Over the past year, he'd come to look forward to Sundays when the whole community had dinner together after church meetings. Lonnie didn't insert himself into the women's conversations, of course, but he loved hearing the musical sound of their voices as they talked and interacted with each other. He couldn't wait for the day that one of those mysterious, animated creatures would be his.

Rachael wasn't animated, but she sure was mysterious. He hadn't realized how poorly she felt until they got to the trading post, and she turned down Marla's invitation to supper. He had looked forward to the supper since the day he got her letter. All the other fellas shared supper at the Doddses the days their women arrived. Adam and Eliza Waring even got hitched at their first supper. It had become a tradition Lonnie wanted to be part of. Of course, Rachael didn't know that. She'd been too tired and wore out to think about sitting around a table chatting with strangers. He guessed he didn't blame her, but he sure was disappointed. He hoped after she rested some, he'd see more of her personality.

He knocked off the sharp edges of the slab of wood with sandpaper, then planed down a smooth, rounded edge.

"Hullo?" came a voice from the door of the shop.

Lonnie continued to smooth down the wood as he went around the corner to see who had come in. Rase Canfield closed the door behind him and unwound a scarf from around his neck. The smithy stayed warm when Lonnie had the forge lit. It was wonderful this time of year but pure torture in the heat of summer. He set the sandpaper and length of wood on the workbench and dusted his hands on the seat of his pants. "Morning, Rase."

"Nice morning out there. Looks like we might get some sunshine."

"That'll be a nice change."

Rase wagged his head toward the workbench. "What you working on there?"

Lonnie looked at the slab of wood. "Little project I thought of last night." He knew Rase must have a reason for riding into town. "Can I do something for you?"

Rase hooked his thumbs in his belt. "Well, actually, it was a nice morning and my curiosity got the better of me. I thought I'd stop in to see how things went yesterday with the new woman."

Lonnie was taken aback. Was Rase interested in a bride? Every time the topic came up, he made it clear he wasn't interested in marriage. A man was entitled to change his mind, though, especially after seeing the difference the women had made in the lives of everyone else in Cowboy Creek.

"Stage was late as usual. Sure was cold waiting. It was nearly dark by the time I got her here."

Rase chuckled. "I appreciate that, but what I meant was how'd it go with *her*. How is she?"

Lonnie hadn't figured out the answer to that question himself. She wasn't what he expected, but he wasn't sure what he'd expected either. Someone more like his mother, he guessed. Meek. Gentle. An easy smile for everyone. Maybe Rachael was all those things, and he hadn't seen it yet. He wasn't sure he wanted to tell any of that to Rase.

"Why you asking? You decide to send for a bride yourself."

Rase grunted. "You know me better than that. I like my life just the way it is."

"Famous last words."

Rase cocked his head as if he knew Lonnie was evading the question. "So what's she like? You think she'll fit in with the other brides?"

And with you, Lonnie knew Rase wanted to add.

He took the piece of wood from the workbench and flicked away a splinter with his thumbnail. "She wasn't feeling well after her trip. Didn't have a whole lot to say on the way here. She didn't stay for supper with Preach and Marla."

"Did you learn anything about her?"

"Not a whole lot. She grew up in a small town before moving to Cincinnati. She's intelligent. We talked about…Shakespeare."

Rase nearly choked. "Shakespeare? Boy, howdy. You got you a fancy gal."

Lonnie shrugged lightly. He didn't want Rase to see his growing uncertainty. "I don't know about that. We were just talking."

"Are you going to Preach and Marla's for supper again tonight?"

"Probably not. They fed me last night. Thought I'd give Rachael—that's her name, Rachael Zeldin—thought I'd give her a day or two to get her bearings. Don't want to make a pest of myself."

"You sure that's a good idea? She may think you're not interested. Women like to think you'd walk through fire to get to them. They got all these romantic notions about knights and gladiators. Expect every man they meet to be one."

Lonnie laughed. "You sure know a lot about women for a man who ain't interested in one."

Rase held up his hands. "Aw, I don't know that much. I'm just sticking my nose in where it doesn't belong."

❀ ❀ ❀

Blessed warmth from the sun pressed down on Rachael's back as she swung the long-handled knife through a stubborn pumpkin vine. Her back ached from the last hour of bending over the vines and toting the pumpkins to the end of the row to gather later.

After the last few days of dreary weather, she reveled in the sun's warmth. Yesterday Marla asked if she wanted to help make pumpkin butter this morning. Everything else in the garden had been harvested a few weeks ago, but pumpkins lingered on the vine. It was good work though, Marla said. Once the pumpkins were brought inside, they would cut and dice all day and then cook down the pumpkin. Tonight, after all the work was done and the beautiful jars of pumpkin butter were lined up on the shelf like golden soldiers, they'd have a nice supper, then roast the pumpkin seeds in butter and cinnamon in the oven.

"Perhaps you can go up and invite Lonnie," Marla had said, eyebrows arched hopefully. "He loves my pumpkin butter."

Rachael had merely smiled in return. She knew what was expected of her. She had come here to marry, and Lonnie was the only eligible bachelor left. She had nothing against the man. He seemed very nice. She was just waiting for a spark. A knot in the pit of her stomach like she had the first time Edwin directed his effervescent smile at her in the shop.

Each week, Edwin's visits got longer and longer as he sought her out to chat. Not just flattering words like Justine and Beatrice warned her against, but also on topics and issues facing the city. He seemed to take her opinions to heart. He was so smart and worldly and interesting. She could talk to him all day. When he invited her for coffee at the end of her shift, she didn't hesitate, despite her coworkers' warnings ringing in her ears. She wasn't a child. Edwin wasn't the first man to pay her attention. She thought she was so sagacious, no one would ever get anything over on her. What a vain fool she'd been.

She wrapped an arm around a pumpkin the size of her head and slowly straightened. She put her free hand to the small of her back and stretched. She was already tired, and she still had a long day ahead of her.

Today was Friday. At the end of every Friday in the shop, she was also tired and more than a little stressed. Women buzzed in all day with their daughters who looked down their perfect little noses at Rachael to pick up dresses for parties and events over the weekend. Fridays were spent finding orders in the back, requesting last minute alterations and adjustments from the designers, and soothing customers who couldn't believe the ensemble they ordered on Monday was the same one they were carrying out of the shop on Friday.

She sighed. Instead of handling silk, lace, and tulle and placating society ladies, she was breaking her dirt encrusted fingernails on pumpkin vines. She turned her face to the sun and breathed in the scent of earth and falling leaves. The change wasn't as bad as she thought. She missed the city. She missed beautiful clothes and swept streets and the praise she received from Mrs. Finnegan and others like her. But this was nice too. She had no idea what her future held here, or even if her future was here, but it was nice to have to think no further than supper tonight with Marla and Preach. And Lonnie.

"I think this is the last of them," Marla said from behind her. She stood with her feet planted wide, a large pumpkin clasped to her midsection. Rachael set the knife and her own pumpkin on the ground and stepped over the withering vines. "Let me take that," she admonished. "It's too big."

"Are you kidding? I've been lifting heavier things than this since before you were in pigtails."

Rachael laughed. "But I'm not in pigtails anymore." She took the pumpkin and grunted under the weight. She cradled the enormous pumpkin against her and lumbered to the end of the row. She bypassed the pumpkins they had already cut and carried it directly to the cutting table Preach had set up this morning. No use putting it down only to pick it up again.

Marla hurried along behind her, carrying smaller pumpkins in each hand. She set them down, then helped Rachael heft the big one onto the table. She gave it a smack. It made a nice hollow sound.

"We had a lot of rain this year, which is good news for pumpkins. We'll get a lot of butter and pies and bread. Best get to it." She slapped the pumpkin again and laughed.

Her enthusiasm rubbed off on Rachael who laughed too, despite the work ahead of them. Work was what she needed. Work to keep her mind off her broken heart while she sorted out her thoughts.

After finishing his chores in the barn, Preach joined them. He took over Marla's role, and Marla disappeared into her living quarters. Soon, Rachael's hands and arms ached from cutting through the heavy pumpkin skins. She nearly shouted for joy when Marla reappeared and announced the noon meal was ready.

By late afternoon a row of pint jars of pumpkin butter and larger jars of canned pumpkin stood cooling on the sideboard. Rachael had nearly decided she never wanted to see another pumpkin, but she stirred with vigor a bubbling mixture for pies for supper. Marla brought a basket out of the other room and lined it with a towel. She set three jars of still-warm pumpkin butter into the basket and carefully nestled the ends of the towel around the jars.

"What are you doing there?" Preach asked.

"It's a downright sin to keep this bounty to ourselves while leaving others to do without. I figured Rachael could carry a few jars to the smithy. You know how Lonnie loves my pumpkin butter. Every time I give him a jar, he acts like it's the first time he tasted it."

"Girl, Lonnie'll be happy to see you coming."

Rachael dipped her hands in the pan of water to wash off the sticky mixture. "Don't forget to invite him down for supper," Marla reminded her. "After the pie, he can stay for singing and the pumpkin seed roast."

"I won't forget." Rachael reached for her heavy shawl. It was still a few hours before sundown, but once the sun began to set, the temperature cooled quickly.

Chapter Six

With the basket in one hand, Rachael held her shawl around her shoulders with the other and picked her way between the muddy patches of melted snow that dotted the street to the smithy. The only sound she heard as she walked was the clink of the jars in the basket and the rush of the river. She looked through the bare trees toward the water as it came in and out of view between the trees. She could see beauty in this place, but the stillness filled her with melancholy.

She enjoyed getting to know Preach and Marla. She appreciated their kindness and generosity. Their easy banter with one another reminded her of Papa and Mama and helped fill the void from losing them. But they weren't the reason she was here. She was here to marry. Every time she thought of marriage, her heart ached anew over Edwin's rejection. Would Lonnie or anyone else ever fill that void?

The rhythmic sound of a hammer on an anvil reached her ears. She shifted the heavy basket to her other arm and followed the sound around the side of the smithy to a door that had been left open a crack.

"Hello," she called as she pushed open the door. The hammering continued unabated. Lonnie stood at a workbench over a small anvil with his back to the door. He held a piece of metal with a pair of heavy black tongs and pounded on it.

Rachael caught the rhythm of the swings and waited until his arm was on the upward motion to call out again. He stopped, hammer in midair, and looked over his shoulder. He quickly set down the tongs and the hammer and pulled a rag out of his back pocket. "Been here long? I didn't hear you." He mopped his forehead and scrubbed at his hands as he came toward her. The pleasure of seeing her was all over his face.

"I just walked in." She motioned with the basket. "Marla wanted you to know we finished the pumpkin butter. She says you always look forward to it."

His smile widened into a gap-toothed grin. "Oh, that woman. She knows the way to my heart." His eyes widened slightly as if realizing what he said. "I haven't had anything as good as her pumpkin butter since my dear ma took sick."

"She said you say that every year."

"I reckon I do." He took the basket out of her hands. "I was ready for a break. I baked a batch of biscuits this morning. They sure would go down a lot easier with Marla's pumpkin butter."

"You bake?"

"I've been a bachelor my whole life. Didn't have no choice but learn my way around a kitchen. Would you care to join me?"

She hesitated only a moment. "I would like that very much."

His eyebrows arched as if he hadn't been sure what to expect from her response. "Let me show you to the kitchen."

Rachael followed him through a well-ordered shop to a door that led into a small kitchen. Through the kitchen door she had a partial view of a parlor. Like the kitchen, it was sparsely furnished with no wall hangings or bric-a-brac. It was tidy and well cared for. The back door in the kitchen had a small window framed by hammered black metal. He led her to a narrow table with two chairs under a large window. The window was framed by the same hammered metal and looked out over the creek. She doubted a body would ever tire of working in this room as long as they had that window to look out. The polished wood floor was void of rugs but stained a pretty blond sheen that brightened the white-washed walls.

"This is a lovely kitchen, Lonnie."

He laughed at her expression. "What were you expecting? A cave with a hole cut in the roof?"

"No...well, maybe."

They both laughed. He set the basket on the table and motioned for her to take a seat. He moved to the stove and set the kettle over the hot plate. He set two cups— porcelain she was surprised to see—on the table along with a basket wrapped in a gingham towel. He peeled back the towel to reveal a mound of golden brown, perfectly shaped biscuits.

"Lonnie, are you sure a woman doesn't live here?" Rachael pretended to look around as though expecting a housekeeper to step out from behind a curtain.

He smiled. "Just me. I wasn't exactly honest when I said I learned to cook because I was a bachelor my whole life. I actually learned long before that. I was the youngest of thirteen. I had a handful of sisters who doted on me and kept me close when I was a little thing. They'd set me up at the kitchen counter while they were kneading biscuits or cracking eggs and put me to work. They said it was to keep me out of mischief. So I learned my way around the kitchen early on. Even before Ma's arthritis forced me to take over much of her work, I was a pretty good hand in the kitchen. When I was grown, I'd work for Pa all day in the foundry, then come home and help Ma fix supper, which always included biscuits."

Rachael broke the seal on one of the pumpkin butter jars. "I'll have to see for myself if your biscuits taste as good as they look."

Once the coffee was hot, he filled the cups and joined her at the table. Rachael split open a biscuit, broke off a piece, and popped it in her mouth. "My, this is perfect."

"You should try them fresh out of the oven."

"I'll have to do that. For now, I'll try them with some of this delicious smelling pumpkin butter. I have to admit I already tried the pumpkin butter. Marla and I had multiple taste tests while we were cooking it."

"That's the best part of cooking." He slathered so much on his biscuit it ran over the side and onto his fingers. He unapologetically licked it away and made an appreciative *um um* before taking a huge bite of biscuit.

They each ate a biscuit in silence. As Lonnie prepared a second one, he asked; "What type of work did you do back in the city?"

She wiped her sticky fingers on a napkin and avoided his gaze as thoughts of Edwin flooded through her. "I worked in a dress shop."

"You make dresses?"

"Not really. Mostly, I was a clerk. I did finish work and the tasks the more experienced workers didn't have time for. I wanted to become a designer eventually. Instead, I waited on customers, took orders and measurements, and made small repairs. I designed hats for a few personal clients in my free time. I enjoy that most of all. My dream was to learn everything I could about hat design." She swept the crumbs off the table into her hand and brushed them onto the plate.

"Your mother and sisters taught you to work in the kitchen. Well, my mother loved to dress pretty. We didn't have much money. You wouldn't have known it by the way my sister and I dressed. Our small town didn't have any nice stores to buy fancy clothes even if we'd had the money. But Mama could turn a simple straw hat into a work of art. I think I got my eye for design from her. She taught us girls how to use a scrap of ribbon or piece of lace or a little extra material to add a sash or cap sleeves on a pinafore to transform a plain outfit into something to behold."

"I reckon it would, though to be honest I have no idea what a pinafore is. Is that anything like a pianoforte?"

She laughed. "No, a pianoforte is a musical instrument. A pinafore is a…oh, Lonnie, you're teasing me."

He smiled back. Warmth shone in his brown eyes. Rachael pursed her lips. He was almost handsome when he smiled like that. It softened the harsh planes on his cheeks and chin. She lowered her eyes, nearly overcome with sadness. He deserved a woman who loved him from the beginning, not one who had to talk herself into being attracted to him.

They talked a little more about childhood and Lonnie's four brothers who had just as much influence on his growing up as the eight sisters. After they drained second cups of coffee, Rachael told him she needed to get back to the trading post. The kitchen was a disaster from canning the pumpkin and she needed to help Marla clean.

"That reminds me," Lonnie said as he followed her to her feet. "I have something for you."

"For me?"

He folded Marla's towel and set it in the basket. He hooked the basket over one arm and motioned her to follow him back to the workshop. He led her to a workbench against a wall. He set the basket on the bench and began brushing at something Rachael couldn't see around him. Finally, he turned and held out a long strip of polished wood. "I made this for you."

Rachael gasped. She took the strip of wood out of his hands to examine it. It was a coatrack with four black hammered, scalloped hooks "Oh, my, Lonnie, this is lovely." She tried to hand it back. "I couldn't take it. It's too nice. You could sell it for a lot of money."

He held up his hands. "I don't want to sell it. I want you to have it. Last night at the brides' house I saw you didn't have anywhere to hang your cloak. I didn't want any harm to come to it. The next time it gets wet, you can hang it on the wall to dry instead of ruining it inside the wardrobe."

He had noticed she had a need without her saying anything. Amazing! "Well, it's very thoughtful. Thank you. I love it."

"I'm glad." His gaze said more than words could.

How completely different this man was from Edwin. In more ways than just the outside. "Thank you again. I won't have to worry about snagging my things on a nail."

"That's what I thought."

The door to the blacksmith shop swung open. A tall man with incredibly wide shoulders stepped inside. Lonnie stuck the coatrack into the basket and turned toward the door.

The tall man held up two wagon wheels, one severely bent, the other only slightly out of round. "I meant to get with you a couple months ago, but we were so busy with growing season, and then harvest, time got away from me." He noticed Rachael and nodded at her.

Rachael tried not to gape. The man had thick dark hair that curled slightly over his ears and a pair of beguiling brown eyes that lit up his perfectly chiseled features.

"Hey, Travis, this is Rachael Zeldin. Rachael, meet Travis Lindell."

Travis nodded his hat at her since his hands were full. "Ma'am."

"Um, er, yes."

"You're from Cincinnati, too, huh?"

"Um, uh, yes."

"You'll have to talk to my wife Scarlett. She got here with her sister at the end of the summer. She doesn't say it much, but I know she misses the city."

Rachael repressed a sigh. What was wrong with her? It was as if she'd lost the ability to form a cohesive sentence at the sight of a good-looking man. "I would imagine." She looped the basket over her arm. "Well, it was nice seeing you—er, meeting you." She glanced at Lonnie who wore a resigned expression.

She fixed her eyes on the floor and hurried past Travis to the door. She felt terrible. She didn't mean to hurt Lonnie's feelings after he had been so kind to her. The nicest man in the world and she made him feel inferior the instant a handsome man crossed her path. She didn't know if there was any way to undo it so she scurried away like a frightened rabbit.

She was nearly to the road when she realized she had forgotten to invite him to supper. She was too embarrassed to go back. They would think she wanted to get another look at Travis. Or was a complete imbecile for forgetting in the first place. She was a crumb who couldn't see beyond good looks and a thick head of hair to appreciate a truly kind and honorable man.

Chapter Seven

Lonnie had seen that look on women's faces his whole life. He couldn't decide which was worse. When they ignored him completely. Or when they offered begrudging attention until a man like Travis walked through the door and Lonnie went right back to being invisible.

He had hoped things would be different with Rachael. She had warmed up since yesterday when she'd been too road-weary for more than a few words. They shared a few laughs over coffee and biscuits and got along well. She liked his baking and had been impressed by the tidy condition of his house. She probably hadn't expected much from a grizzled old bachelor. She even looked at him as if she didn't notice he wasn't handsome. That meant more to Lonnie than anything.

That all changed when Travis walked in. The problem for men like Lonnie was there was a Travis in every crowd. Lonnie wasn't envious or angry. He'd accepted years ago it was just the way things were. Truth be told, he was proud of his looks—if a man could take pride in such a thing. He looked like Pa, and Pa was the greatest man he ever knew. He just wished there was a woman who recognized it too. For a few hours there, he thought Rachael might be that woman.

Apparently not.

All evening Rachael agonized over her reaction to seeing Travis. He caught her by surprise was all. If she had seen him from a distance or in a church pew next to his wife, she wouldn't have behaved like a silly schoolgirl. Regardless of her inappropriate behavior, she needed to apologize to Lonnie. But how did one apologize for such a thing without insulting the offended party further?

She begged off the pumpkin seed roast, telling Preach and Marla she was tired and wanted to turn in early.

The next morning she only managed to eat a few bites of breakfast. She'd always had a nervous stomach, especially after doing something stupid. She couldn't stop mulling over how to apologize to Lonnie without making the situation worse. Then it came to her.

Shakespeare.

She excused herself from the table, telling Marla she wasn't feeling well and hurried across the street to the makeshift library made up with Bridget DeSantis's books. Marla had told her it was an extensive collection. Surely there was something by Shakespeare to share with Lonnie. If he didn't have time or an interest in reading, it would at least give her a reason to talk to him without reminding him how rude she'd been.

The light was dim inside the building. It took nearly thirty minutes of searching before she found a collection of stories by the illustrious poet and playwright. She wrote her name and the book title in the ledger on the table. After depositing the book in the brides' house, she hurried back to the trading post to talk to Marla.

Marla stood at the counter with a pot of minced pumpkin. "Are you feeling better?"

"Yes, thank you." She couldn't admit what had upset her stomach in the first place. "Is there enough pumpkin left that we could bake a few pies to share at the church dinner tomorrow."

Marla wagged her head at the kettle she was preparing. "I suppose we could share a little."

Rachael smiled appreciatively. "And maybe we could make an extra one that I could take to Lonnie. I feel terrible about forgetting to invite him to supper last night."

Marla sighed happily. Rachael knew what the older woman was thinking—that she was falling in love with the blacksmith. She didn't know if she'd fall in love again. She just wanted to show him he didn't deserve to be dismissed like she'd done yesterday.

"That's a wonderful idea," Marla said. "How about you take charge of the crusts this time." She quickly set out ingredients. "I so enjoy having help in the kitchen again. Candace Whitamore comes down and helps me whenever her mother doesn't need her. My, my, I do love that girl. I love all of them, of course. But it's nice to have another woman to talk to while I work. Reminds me of when I was a girl. There were sixteen of us children."

Rachael's eyes bulged. "Sixteen!"

Marla laughed. "I was somewhere in the middle. By the time I got old enough to be much help, some of the older ones were grown and gone. There was always a little one to cuddle. And so many mouths to cook for between cousins and grandparents and hired hands milling about. Plenty of times we had to eat in shifts. That meant we girls spent the entire day in the kitchen or garden, chopping, cleaning, and stirring. Then the cleanup afterward."

She let out an exaggerated sigh. "My, my, I thought the work would never end. It wasn't fair either. The boys worked outside in the sunshine. Their work ended once the sun went down. Not ours. Even on rainy days or in the middle of a blizzard when the men didn't have work to do, we girls had to keep everyone fed. And, land's sakes, the wash! Imagine keeping twenty people in clean drawers."

She shuddered, then burst out laughing. Rachael laughed, too, at the audacity of the statement. She'd never met anyone who talked like Marla, or who openly lamented the washing of undergarments.

Marla sobered and brushed at her damp eyes with the back of her hand. "Sometimes I think I'd like to go back to those days. Just for a day or two, mind you. The laughing, the complaining, the sore backs and chapped hands. Despite how hard the work or how tired we got, we had fun. My sister Ruth loved to sing. She'd get a song going, and we'd all join in, even the boys. We were a very musical family. Our grandmother had a piano. That's where I learned to play.

"We'd sing and laugh and talk while we worked. Having you brides here reminds me of those days. Our last harvest was the best one we ever had. Not just because of the crops we put up, but because I had those ladies keeping me company. Didn't seem like work at all. Not one day of it. I thought those days were behind me. The Lord has been good to me in my old age."

She took her hands out of the bowl where she'd been mashing sugar and cinnamon into the pumpkin puree. She faced Rachael without wiping them off since she wasn't finished. "You know you can tell me anything, girl. There isn't a thing that's happened I haven't heard before."

Rachael's fork moved faster and faster as she cut lard into the flour mixture. "I...um...don't know what you mean." Surely Lonnie hadn't said anything to Marla about her ogling Travis. Marla was intuitive and she thought the world of Lonnie. If she thought Rachael had intentionally hurt him, she would take Rachael to task. Not to mention, Travis was a married man. There was no way Marla would stand back and let Rachael make eyes at another woman's husband.

"Nothing's wrong, Marla. The pumpkin harvesting got my back stiffened up." She wasn't exactly lying. Her back was a trifle sore. "I didn't sleep well. I woke up a little headachy."

Marla finished the puree and went to the sink to wash her hands. When she finished, she stayed at the sink rubbing the towel between each finger. "What do you think of Lonnie?"

Rachael's stomach dropped. She knew. But how? She was sure Lonnie wasn't a talebearer. She didn't know if he'd even been that offended by her reaction to Travis. Then she remembered their conversation when she took him the pumpkin butter. Maybe that's what Marla meant.

"He's very nice. Did you know he's read Shakespeare? A little, anyway. And he's such a good housekeeper. I found that quite surprising."

Marla nodded, knowingly. "Lonnie is a surprising person. There's much more to him than meets the eye."

As Rachael was quickly finding out.

She pushed the rolling pin over the pie crust so she wouldn't see Marla's measuring gaze. "He's funny too. I've enjoyed getting to know him."

"I'm glad. He deserves someone who can see the gem under his rough exterior." Marla set two pie tins next to the finished crusts.

Rachael heard what Marla wasn't saying. Lonnie was a good man, and she didn't want him to get hurt. Rachael understood that, but she was still holding out for a spark. She wanted a man who lit up her world at the thought of him. After the fiasco with Edwin, she doubted such a man existed. Coming here might've been a bad decision. Lonnie was so kind and thoughtful. She didn't want to use him, but what choice did she have? If this didn't work out, she had nowhere else to go.

Her stomach roiled at her whirling thoughts. Even if she didn't love Lonnie, she didn't want to leave. She already liked Cowboy Creek. She liked Lonnie. She cared for Marla and Preach. They might not care so much for her if they found out what type of person she truly was.

Vegetables were bubbling on the stove when Marla thrust the fresh pie into Rachael's hands. "Take this up the hill while it's still warm. Tell Lonnie supper will be ready in a little while if he wants to join us, unless you'd rather eat there with him. Knowing him, he's probably got a pot of beans cooking."

Rachael turned away so Marla wouldn't see the flush on her cheeks. She wasn't sure Lonnie would want to share his beans with her. She fastened her cloak around her shoulders, pulled up the hood—more to hide her embarrassment than for the warmth—and headed out the door. Her stomach churned as she trudged up the hill to the blacksmith shop.

The large bay door was closed. She circled the building to the side door. She maneuvered the pie against her side so she could turn the knob. The shop was empty. The fire in the foundry had died down but the building was still warm despite the temperature outside. She took a few steps into the building and called out. "Lonnie? Hello? Anyone home?"

She heard a chair scrape against the floor from his living quarters. Lonnie appeared in the doorway. His suspenders were off his shoulders and hung loose around his narrow hips. His thin hair was wet as if it had just been washed and was combed neatly against his scalp. The scent of bergamot soap wafted toward her over the smell of the cinnamon and clove from the pie. For the first time Rachael noticed the width of his shoulders and the outline of his forearms and biceps straining against the fabric of his shirt. The rippling muscles had been duly earned from a lifetime of swinging a hammer. Her mouth went dry.

"Um, we thought…Marla thought…you might like…" She sighed and started over. "Marla and I baked a few pies for the dinner tomorrow. She said it's been a good year for pumpkin. We wanted to bring you this. I hope you like pumpkin," she added, stupidly. Of course he liked pumpkin. Hadn't he lost his mind over the pumpkin butter?

He smiled and his brown eyes gleamed. He seemed pleased by her discomfort. Rachael bit down on her top lip. She deserved it.

"It's my favorite," he said. "That and apple and blackberry and cherry and whatever else is in season."

Rachael smiled appreciatively. "Mine too."

His hands brushed hers as he took the pie from her. A charge shot through her, startling her. When Edwin smiled at her, touched her, kissed her, she'd felt the same jolt of pleasure, but she recognized now it had been immature, based on false flattery and self-interest. From Lonnie, it seemed genuine. Was this the spark she'd been waiting for?

She realized Lonnie was staring down at her. She hadn't yet released her hold on the pie. "Oh, sorry," she murmured.

He didn't seem to mind. He turned in the doorway and went into the kitchen. Rachael followed. He set the pie on the table next to a pan of cornmeal batter. As Marla suspected, a pot of beans bubbled on the stove. "I was just about to put a batch of cornbread in the oven. Won't take long? Would you like to stay? We can have your pie for dessert."

"No. I mean…Marla told me to invite you for supper. I was supposed to yesterday but…" She stopped talking. She'd been so flustered at the sight of Travis, all thoughts of a supper invitation had flown out of her head. "Also, I wanted to thank you again for the coatrack. I nailed it up last night. It's beautiful and just perfect for my cloak and coat. The wardrobe is nice, but it's small and cramped. I appreciate not having to crush the cloak."

One corner of his mouth tilted upward as he watched her talk. Rachael stared at him, noting how the mischievous gleam in his eye made him look younger and rakish. She quickly glanced away. He must think her silly and immature for staring at every man who crossed her path "She's cooking a pork roast and vegetables for tomorrow, but there's enough for supper tonight as well."

Lonnie leaned his hips against the table and crossed his arms over his chest. "Marla certainly knows her way around a pork roast." He looked down at the unbaked cornbread. "I need to go ahead and bake this first. My ma would wear me out if she knew I wasted perfectly good food."

Rachael tried not to notice the picture of masculinity he presented with his hip cocked and his chest thrust out. He seemed completely unaware. Maybe he was. Edwin had known just how to stand and smile and present himself for maximum effect depending on his audience.

"The cornbread would go well with Marla's roast, or you can save it for later."

The corner of his mouth quirked again as he gave her a measuring look. Did he know the path her mind had taken? She thought he was inexperienced with women, but he sure seemed aware of how discomfited she was now.

He pushed off the table and slid the pan into the oven. He set the coffeepot on one of the stove's hot plates. "We can have some coffee while we wait. We can cut into this pie if you like."

Rachael's stomach clenched in response. "No, thanks. I've done enough taste-testing as it is the last two days."

"Then I'll eat the whole thing myself later unless you'd like to come up after dinner tomorrow and share a piece."

She smiled, relieved he didn't seem perturbed by the way she acted yesterday. "I'll think about it."

Chapter Eight

Rachael hadn't been to church since the day she spoke to Nan Canfield about coming to Cowboy Creek. Even before then, her church attendance was sporadic at best. Sundays were her only day off. She always had so many things to take care of before going back to Mr. Winegard's shop on Monday. It was also the only day she had time to work on her own projects for her growing list of clients. The one item on her agenda she could forego was church attendance.

According to Preach, everyone in Cowboy Creek attended the services at the meetinghouse. He said in the dead of winter only the worst of conditions kept people away. He laughed and explained his sermons weren't the big draw, but the chance to get together with neighbors and away from the monotony of daily life.

Though the weather was still cold and dreary on her first Sunday, there had been no additional snowfall or other calamities to keep people at home. It looked like Rachael would get to meet the entire community in one fell swoop. She was anxious to talk with the women. Not one of them had run back to Nan Canfield regretting her decision to leave the city, so the arrangement to bring brides to the ranchers had obviously been a success.

Last night she had taken her best dress out of the crowded wardrobe to shake out the wrinkles. Now she dressed carefully and took extra care styling her hair. She wasn't sure who she was dressing up for other than herself. She liked beautiful things—clothes, shoes, hair pieces, and especially hats. It wouldn't be hard to impress Lonnie. She saw on his face the day she arrived that he was pleased with her, and she had looked a fright that day.

The wind outside pulled forcefully at the eaves. She picked up her hat, then put it back in the hatbox and replaced the lid. Hatboxes took up too much space in her luggage, so she'd given most of her hats away before heading west. This one was her favorite. She didn't want to risk chasing it down the muddy street if the wind caught hold of it. Instead, she carefully lifted the hood of her velvet cloak over her coiffed hair and headed outside. Even without a hat, the wind fought her. She pulled hard on the warped door of the brides' house to get outside, then struggled again to secure it shut behind her. She hurried past the barn to have breakfast with Preach and Marla before going to the meetinghouse.

"Rachael," came a voice from behind her.

The slope of the hills was propelling Lonnie toward her. One hand was clapped over his hat to keep it from sailing away. Her heart did a little lurch. She wasn't sure what it meant. Surely she wasn't falling for this bow-legged blacksmith after less than a week. Not that long ago, she thought she loved Edwin. He was everything she thought she wanted in a man. Now she realized he was nothing more than an empty suit. Plain Lonnie with his soot-stained fingernails was showing her what a man should be, and her heart was reacting.

She hunched her shoulders against the wind and waited. "What are you doing out so early?" she asked when he caught up with her. "Church doesn't start for another hour."

He grabbed at the tail of her cloak flapping in the wind and tightened it around her. "It's my turn to come early and light the fire in the building."

"How thoughtful," she said. The wind snatched her words away. He was thoughtful. Not only to a woman whose attention he hoped to capture but to everyone.

"Not thoughtful. Necessary."

She wrapped her arms around herself. "I'll help you."

He looked down at her velvet cloak and the black boots sticking out from underneath. "Nah. I don't want you to ruin your clothes. And that meetinghouse is colder than the bottom of a mineshaft before the fire gets going."

"I don't mind," she burst out before she could stop herself. She did mind. She hated the cold. But she liked Lonnie. She wasn't sure why. He wasn't the type of man she usually took note of.

"If I can't help, I'll keep you company. Afterward, you can come over to Preach and Marla's to warm up."

"Best idea I've heard all morning." He grabbed her gloved hand and they half-ran to the meetinghouse. Inside they were out of the wind, but Lonnie was right; it was just as cold inside the drafty old building as out.

She followed him to the stove in the middle of the room. She hunched her shoulders and pulled her cloak tighter around her. "Are the winters always this cold?"

He chuckled as he set about laying a pyramid of sticks from the kindling box. "Winter? It's only November. We're a whole month away from winter."

She shivered for effect. "Oh, right, November. I keep forgetting. Are you saying this is nothing compared to January or February?"

He laughed outright. "Nothing at all. You'll see." He glanced at her from under the brim of his hat.

Would she? Would she be here in January or February? She looked down at the small stack of wood so she wouldn't have to look at him. "Shall I bring in more firewood?"

He glanced critically down the length of her velvet cloak. He shook his head. "You're only here to keep me company, remember? I don't want you to ruin those fancy, city-girl duds."

"Don't say I didn't offer."

He grinned in response. Rachael watched him work. She rocked side to side to keep her blood circulating. "Do you do this every Sunday?"

"Pretty near. Preach or me, either one. The other fellas have offered, but it isn't necessary with them living so far out. I'm a quick ride down the hill. I usually get it going, then go back home for breakfast or I beg something off Marla."

Rachael smiled. "Marla seems like a surrogate mother to everybody."

"She is at that. Back when everyone else was hightailing it outta here, she and Preach came to ask me if I was leaving, too, or staying put."

He lit a piece of paper and shoved it into the pyramid of narrow sticks. He fanned it with his hand and watched to make sure the flame took.

"Why did you stay? Couldn't you make a better living in a bigger town." He would've had a better chance at meeting a woman, too, but she didn't say that part out loud. "My coatrack is lovely. In a bigger town, you could've set up a shop next to your smithy and sold all sorts of things."

He blew gently on the budding flame. "I reckon I could've." He added a handful of dried bark and leaves and slivers of wood. He straightened and reached for a larger piece.

"Then why didn't you? Why choose to stay here? Even with people moving in, it's so…lonely."

He stopped what he was doing to stare at her. "You think it's lonely?"

"Yes. No," she amended. "I don't know. Maybe after I get to know everyone…" She shrugged.

He reached across the stove and tugged free a cobweb caught in her hair. "You know me." He kept his hand suspended between them.

Suddenly the room felt close. And warm. Rachael's arms went all prickly inside her cloak. "Yes, I know you." She couldn't think of anything else to say, and it seemed like she needed to say something.

He dropped his hand and grinned. She felt her eyes widen. He was handsome when he smiled like that. Not handsome in the traditional sense, but warm and intelligent. Appealing was the best word to describe him. She hated that she was so surprised by the revelation. Had she always been so petty?

"And I know you," he said with an intimate smile, "so I reckon I'll stay put."

He continued to stare. Rachael clasped her hands around her arms, uncomfortable at his perusal but liking it at the same time. She coughed. A finger of black smoke curled out of the seam of the stovepipe.

Lonnie noticed the smoke. "Uh oh. Better take care of that." He wrapped both hands around the pipe and twisted gently to fit it back into place. The bottom half of the pipe shifted. The finger of black smoke turned into a stream. He got a tighter hold on the pipe and twisted again. "You need to step back before—"

A rip appeared between his hands in the corrugated pipe. It came apart as easily as a rip in a sheet of paper. Black smoke mushroomed into the room. Rachael shrieked and jumped backward as soot and ash rained down over them like fine mist. Lonnie screwed his face up tight against the smoke and soot. The soot quickly settled, but a gray cloud remained. Rachael lowered her hands where she had tried to protect herself. She looked down at her beautiful cape. It was covered in black ash. "Oh, no!"

She coughed. She wanted to cry at the black soot that covered them, the floor, and the circle of chairs around the stove. At least she hadn't worn her favorite hat and ruined it too.

Lonnie opened his eyes. "Oh, Rachael, your cloak. I should've sent you out before I checked the pipe. I'm so sorry."

Rachael looked at him still holding half of the busted pipe in his hands. His hat, hair, face, and clothes were coated with black soot. The only parts of him not caked in black were the whites of his eyes, his teeth, and the wrinkles around his eyes and mouth where he had squinted against the falling ash. She knew she looked just as bad. She burst out laughing.

"What's so funny?" he asked, trying to look offended as laughter spilled out of him.

"You're a mess!" she said around another cough. The longer she looked at him, the harder she laughed. Her sides rocked until they hurt.

His responding rollicking laugh warmed her all the way to her toes. It was a full minute before either of them could do anything but laugh and cough.

She peeled off her blackened gloves and laughed again at the sight of her clean, white hands against her black wrists. "This is terrible. What are we going to do?"

"Jump in the creek?"

"We'd ruin the water supply." She playfully slapped him with one of her gloves in the center of his chest. A black cloud billowed toward her. Fresh peals of laughter erupted from her lips. She had never laughed so hard in her life.

She dragged her fingertips down his face, leaving four white streaks on each cheek.

"You're not helping," he said, still laughing.

"I bet I could write my name on your face."

"You try and I'll empty the rest of this pipe over your head."

"I'll tell Marla."

"I think we're both already in trouble with Marla."

On impulse, she swiped her thumb across his mouth, exposing pink lips. Their laughter died simultaneously as if doused with cold water. Lonnie stared down at her. Rachael stared back, unable to believe what she'd just done. He leaned over the broken half of pipe still clutched in his hands. Rachael thought of her own soot-coated lips, but it didn't keep her from leaning into him. Despite the dirt and grime—or maybe because of it—the kiss was light and sweet. When she pulled back, all mirth had been erased from Lonnie's eyes. She wasn't sure what she was thinking. Except that Lonnie Fanshaw wasn't anything like she expected when he helped her out of the stage in Good Hope. He wasn't like any man she ever met.

"I should…um…tell Marla what happened." She turned in the slippery ash and hurried out of the meetinghouse. It crossed her mind to go back and clarify she didn't mean to tell Marla about the kiss. Surely he figured that part out without her saying so.

Dinner was late that day. After Rachael told Marla and Preach about the busted pipe, Marla filled two buckets with hot water from the stove and followed her to the brides' house while Preach went to the meetinghouse to survey the damage. It took four more buckets of hot water to get the soot out of Rachael's ears and hair. Her beautiful cloak had shielded most of her dress and clothes, but she'd have to replace the collar and sleeve cuffs. Every time Marla poured a bucket of clean water over her head and it ran off black, she laughed all over again. She couldn't get the image of her fingermarks on Lonnie's face out of her head.

Or his soft lips. That thought always stifled her laughter.

By the time she was clean enough to be seen in public, she and Marla had missed Preach's sermon. The women were at the sawhorse tables setting out the food when they got to the meetinghouse.

"What a morning you've had," Katie observed.

"It was terrible," Rachael said laughing as though it wasn't terrible at all. She looked toward the stove. A large clean circle had been scrubbed on the floor, but the ceiling was gray with soot. "I'm sorry for all the work it caused."

Rennie Campbell chuckled. "It was no trouble. Preach and Lonnie had the worst of it cleaned up by the time we got here."

Carrie Whitamore grinned. "Preach said all he could see of Lonnie were the whites of his eyes."

And his lips, Rachael thought guiltily.

She tried to look repentant. "Where is he? Is he still cleaning up? I'm afraid I wasn't very compassionate over his predicament."

The women laughed. "He didn't seem to mind," Scarlett said with a mischievous smile. She nudged her sister Marianne.

Marianne grinned back and returned the nudge. "He had a dazed look in his eyes when Nathan and I saw him headed up the hill. I don't think he'd mind if you set his smithy on fire."

Rachael blushed. She was glad the women didn't know the whole story, though they'd probably deduced enough to know something had happened besides a busted stovepipe.

Lonnie arrived clean and smelling of bergamot soap just as Rase Canfield wrapped up a blessing over the food. Rachael was heartened to see all the men in the community seemed mature in the Lord and didn't leave all the spiritual work like prayer to Preach. Edwin had never mentioned God. For all his talk, she didn't know anything about his spiritual condition. Everything she knew was superficial. He was intelligent, all right. He could discuss politics and literature all day long, but personal topics that might expose the man inside never came up. He was equally disinterested in knowing the real *her*. Edwin had been funny and charismatic. But shallow. He wasn't kind or thoughtful like Lonnie.

How could she have envisioned a future with him? What did it say about her own character?

She filled a plate and found a seat at the table next to an empty chair. As expected, Lonnie dropped into it and set his plate on the table. All thoughts of Edwin evaporated as a cloud of contentment enveloped her.

She swallowed a nervous giggle. She hoped she wouldn't burst out laughing again. "You look much better."

"You too. Listen, I'm sorry about your cloak. I knew that pipe was wearing out. I hadn't changed it in three winters. I should've—"

Rachael dropped her hand on his arm. "Don't. There was no real harm done."

"I'm afraid there was. Your cloak's ruined. I know how much it means to you."

Her heart swelled at the concern in his eyes. "Marla said she might be able to help me clean it. If not, well, it's just a cloak. I do love it, but it's not very practical for Cowboy Creek."

He glanced at her hand on his arm. "Does that mean you might want to stay?"

Was this a proposal? Or a prelude to one? Rachael realized with a start she liked the idea very much. "I think

I would." They stared at each other for a long moment. She pulled her hand loose and picked up her fork.

Lonnie took a deep breath before speaking. She wondered if it was to swallow a lump in his throat like the one in hers. "The next time I go to the city I'll buy you a new cloak."

"I don't want you to do that, Lonnie. It's fine, really. But thank you for worrying about it." She lowered her voice and leaned in close. "No one has worried about me in a long time. It's nice."

And it was.

Chapter Ten

Rachael awoke to the smell of soot in her nose. She barely made it to the chamber pot before emptying her stomach. When she came home from dinner yesterday, the stench had assaulted her as soon as she walked through the door. She finished scrubbing her clothes and hung everything, including the ruined cloak, over the porch railing outside. She prayed for God to close up the skies so it wouldn't rain or snow until her things aired out. Even with her clothes outside, the smell permeated every surface of the little house. Her bedclothes, the walls; everything reeked and turned her stomach.

Even though it was cold outside, she opened the door and windows and began to scrub every surface within reach. She was on her hands and knees scrubbing the floor when a shadow fell across her. She knew without looking it was Lonnie. She could already recognize the shape of his legs and powerful arms, even in shadow. She clamored to her feet and dried her hands as he strode in and closed the door behind him.

Her pulse quickened. "I left the door open to air out the smell. I can't get that stench out of my nose."

He inhaled deeply. "Smells fresh as a daisy in here to me. To a blacksmith, smoke and ash smell like prosperity." He chuckled, then lifted the lid of the stove and threw in a chunk of wood. "I'll get it warm in here in two shakes of a lamb's tail."

Rachael stepped closer to the stove. "I can't keep the fire going with the draft, but I can't stomach the smell either."

"You've cleaned most of the smoke away. I left my dirty clothes in the workshop, so they didn't stink up my house."

"I thought smoke smells like prosperity to you," she teased.

"Yeah, well, a man can take only so much prosperity." He set aside the fire poker. "The sun's out. Looks like we might have more snow by morning. Why don't we take advantage of the sunshine and clear your lungs?"

"More snow? This is the snowiest place I've ever seen. Is every winter like this one?"

"I told you we've still got a full month before winter gets here. Some years are mild and we don't see much white at all. Other years we're buried under a few feet until April. All a man can do is wait and see and be prepared for either. Come on. Get your coat. It'll be warm and toasty and fresh smelling by the time we get back."

He took the coat off the coatrack he'd built and held it open for her. "I saw your cloak hanging over the hitching rail. I'm sorry."

"Stop apologizing, would you? Things wear out and break. And sometimes get covered with ash."

"Maybe so, but what does it say about my skills as a blacksmith when a stovepipe bursts and ruins the inside of the meetinghouse? And your clothes?"

"It says that things happen. No one blames you."

As she buttoned up and put on a clean pair of gloves, he made quick work of closing the windows and turning down the stove flue. He held the door for her and followed her outside. She stepped into a patch of sunshine and realized he was right. Even with patches of snow under the trees and against the buildings, it was warmer outside in the sun than inside the brides' house.

"Have you walked along the creek to where the old gold elevator was?" he asked. "The elevator's mostly given up to the elements, but you can still see the foundation. It was really humming back in Cowboy Creek's heyday. I built much of it. Would you like to see?"

Rachael smiled at him. "I walked past it myself last week, and I had a dozen questions. I'd love a guided tour."

His chest expanded inside his coat. "I can do that."

They reached a slippery, muddy patch on the road. Lonnie took her elbow to help her over. Her foot slipped, and she tightened her grip on his arm. He steadied her and smiled. A warm flush worked its way into her cheeks. Rachael was glad she'd slipped on her leather gloves. She hoped they disguised the trembling in her hands. She didn't remember Edwin making her so uncomfortable. With him, everything was fun and exhilarating. Lonnie was…unsettling.

They reached dry ground, but he kept hold of her arm. "There's a woman in Good Hope who makes quilts and coats and the like. Her husband passed away about ten years ago. She makes a decent living for herself sewing and repairing slipcovers and bedding. If anyone can repair your cloak, it'd be her. I can take it to her tomorrow and have her look at it."

"Marla said she'd help me."

"Let me take care of it, will you? If the lady in Good Hope can't clean it up, I'll bring it back and you and Marla can have a crack at it."

"All right."

A little farther down the road, Lonnie stepped onto a path Rachael noticed the other day but hadn't taken. "This is the easiest route," he explained. "As you can see, it was well traveled, but it's grown up over the last couple of years." They walked deeper into the bare trees. Rachael tightened her hand around his arm as her feet slipped and slid.

Lonnie took her hand, then wrapped his other arm around her. "Just a little farther. It levels off here in a minute."

"Who was the first one to find gold in this stream?"

"Two cowboys, hence the name. Daulton and Uriah Evans. Cousins, I always heard. By the time I got here, they were nothing but a memory. All the good claims were taken. That was all right with me. There was more potential for me in blacksmithing. I built a little blacksmith shop where I am now and hung out my shingle. Those prospectors kept me busy morning and night. Didn't have time to even put a proper roof over my head.

"Like the rest of those who stayed, I loved the land. There's a lot of potential here. I couldn't understand why everyone was so quick to leave when the creek stopped producing. Chasing fantasies and hoping to find the one rock to make you rich didn't seem like much of a life for me. Some of the people here did all right for themselves. But most who struck it rich lost it all in the next go-round. That's how it usually works. Rich one day. Dead broke and chasing it again the next. That wasn't the life I wanted."

"What life did you want?"

He pulled her to a stop. "The same as I had growing up, I suppose. I always imagined doing like my pa and teaching my sons the smithing trade."

"You must've known it wasn't likely to happen in a place as remote as this."

They started walking again. "I put the whole thing in God's hands. I loved this land from the minute I saw it. I love blacksmithing and waking up every morning knowing I can enjoy that view out my front door. If I never get anything else I want, I figure I'm still ahead of a lot of fellas I know. I like what I do, and I like the people I do it for. I wouldn't mind if our little community grew a little. Whether it does or doesn't, I plan to stay right here and be planted in the field above the mill when my time comes."

They reached the water. He pointed to a jetty at the edge of the stream. "The flue came down from there. That's where everyone started work. They'd wash the pans and see what remained."

They picked their way across the wet stones for Rachael to get a better look. Lonnie led her to a flat spot and motioned for her to sit. "This is where the table used to be where they'd run the water through. It fell apart over time and washed downstream. This spot is still nice in the summer. We men like to jump into the pool from here to clean off. Don't reckon we can do that anymore now that womenfolk are here."

He ducked his head sheepishly as if worried he had offended her by talking about bathing. Rachael wasn't offended. She chuckled. "You'll have to find a more secluded spot."

His shoulder occasionally brushed hers as they sat side by side. Rachael wanted to lean against him, but she didn't want to seem forward. She still couldn't get over wiping her finger across his lips yesterday. It had proven more intimate than the kiss.

"What about you, Rachael?" he asked after they watched the water for a few minutes. "Why did you come here?"

Her mind immediately went to Edwin. If she had never gotten involved with him, she wouldn't be sitting here now. Then again, maybe she would. Even if he hadn't broken her heart, she may have decided there was nothing in Cincinnati and gone in search of a different life. She looked downstream. She had never imagined this was what she wanted. Now that she was here, it seemed like what she was born for.

"I…wanted something different." She hoped he wouldn't press for details.

It wasn't exactly a lie. She couldn't keep working at Mr. Winegard's shop after everyone discovered Edwin jilted her and what had led him to do it, but she was afraid to start over somewhere else. It was easier to leave. She couldn't tell Lonnie any of that.

"There had to have been more of a reason than that." It looked like he was going to press.

She stared at the water. She couldn't tell him. He would never understand. "I don't think I liked who I had become there," she answered honestly.

He took hold of her chin and turned her face toward him. "I can't imagine you were ever anything other than smart and extraordinary and beautiful."

She wanted to tell him he didn't know her at all. "Thank you for saying that," she said instead.

"I mean it."

"I know, it's just…I'm not exactly young. I missed my chance for many of the things women dream of."

"Like what?"

"Are you really going to make me say it?"

He looked intently into her eyes. "Yes."

She sighed. "Love."

"If a woman as beautiful as you can't find a man in the city, she isn't trying very hard."

"It isn't that easy, Lonnie. Especially after the flower of youth has faded. A woman develops too many opinions when she's on her own for a while. Men don't like opinions in women. They want a malleable mind they can mold to suit them."

"Is that what you think I want?"

She didn't respond right away, knowing he'd want a complete and thoughtful answer. "You're one of a kind. I doubt there's another man alive like you."

He wrinkled his nose. "I'm not sure if that's a good thing or a bad thing."

Rachael laughed, relieved at the break in tension. "It's a good thing, believe me. I like spending time with you. I don't feel like I have to be something I'm not to impress you."

He pulled back. "Why in the world would you choose to spend time with someone who didn't like you for who you are?"

"I honestly don't know. But I've done it."

He looked toward the water as if weighing her words. She hadn't told him the whole story, but the part she told was the truth. She pulled in her feet to stand. "It's cold, Lonnie. I'm ready to go back."

He stood and helped her to her feet. They had to keep their eyes on their feet as they walked to make sure they didn't stumble or slip on the uneven path. When they reached level ground, Lonnie took her arm and turned her toward him. "I'm sorry you ever had to pretend to be someone you weren't. I'm glad you're here just the way you are."

She looked into his eyes. "I'm glad, too, Lonnie." She saw his intent in his eyes before he lowered his mouth to hers. Rachael's heart seemed to skip a beat at the touch of his lips on hers. The kiss was longer and more intense than in the meetinghouse. She put her hands on his shoulders and pulled closer. She wanted to stay here forever. He was so kind. So good. Her heart raced. There was the spark she'd been waiting for. But she hadn't been completely honest. She only told him enough to garner sympathy, something she didn't deserve. He deserved better than her—a pure woman who could give him what he wanted, not someone who had already made a huge mistake and couldn't build up the nerve to tell the truth.

She pulled away. His eyes bored into hers. "Lonnie," she whispered. His eyes softened. She couldn't trust her feelings. She couldn't hurt him the way Edwin had hurt her. She dropped her hands from his shoulders. "I—I can't."

Confusion replaced the passion in his eyes. He opened his mouth to speak, but she turned and hurried as quickly as she dared across the wet stones to the road and the brides' house.

Lonnie took two running steps after her, then stopped. What was he doing? He wasn't surprised. Not really. Yesterday when they had laughed and laughed, then she brushed her finger across his lips—well, he'd been ready to propose right then. Then she ran out to tell Marla about the mess they'd made. Even if she hadn't, part of him held back. He wanted to believe she was beginning to feel for him the way he felt for her. But he couldn't stop waiting for the hammer to fall and crush that hope.

He remembered his prayers from a few months ago when he first read her letter. She hadn't revealed much in the letter, but he prayed anyway. Then last night as he tried to fall asleep, he wondered if God had answered his prayers. Finally. After all this time.

But no. She didn't feel the same way. He didn't measure up. He never would. He wasn't handsome like Travis or young like Jacob or a natural leader like Rase. He was plain, old Lonnie Fanshaw; his shoulders stooped and fingernails caked with black that wouldn't scrub away. It was part of what had made him who he was. It meant he was hardworking and successful. If a woman couldn't appreciate it, he was better off knowing now.

Rachael disappeared around the corner of the barn. His chest filled with...emptiness. He expected sorrow, but that had come and gone years ago. The only thing left to feel was nothing.

He replayed her words in his head. Suddenly they made sense. She didn't come here because she wanted to. She came because she had nothing else. She didn't want Lonnie—she was only settling for him because she had no other options. And she couldn't even go through with it.

He wouldn't chase her. He had some pride. If he couldn't be a woman's first choice, he wouldn't be her last hope.

Chapter Eleven

Rachael wiped the washcloth across her mouth and stared at her reflection in the mirror. How could she pretend not to see it? The puffy eyes. The sallow skin. The fullness along her jawline. Even if she could willfully overlook those signs, she couldn't ignore how she barely made it out of bed before emptying her stomach. Again.

She'd had her suspicions—her fear—since that night with Edwin. Now the signs wouldn't allow her to remain blissfully ignorant. Her sensitivity to smell. Her upset stomach. Her lack of appetite for foods she previously loved. At first, she blamed missing her monthlies on jangled nerves over losing Edwin. She blamed it on the stress and upheaval of travel, the different surroundings, the strange foods, her broken heart. But the morning after running away from Lonnie, who only wanted to love her, the truth crashed down around her and wouldn't be ignored a moment longer.

For the first few weeks after she spent that evening with Edwin, she feared this result. She knew what happened when men and women came together. It had only been one time. They were safe after only one time. Right? And they loved each other. Even if the worst did happen, she never doubted he would do the right thing. He was an honorable man. All the way home that night, she expected him to ask her to marry him. That's what people did. It was never spoken of, but she wasn't so naïve as to believe relations between unmarried people didn't happen. She'd read the Bible. It happened countless times. It was wrong in God's sight but not an unpardonable sin. They would marry, and if a child resulted from their unlawful union—Oh, God, please don't let it be so—it would be loved and cherished.

Edwin didn't ask her to marry him. He barely even looked at her. The next Monday when he came into the shop, he went directly to Mr. Winegard's office without looking in her direction. Rachael had tried to keep the chagrin off her face, but she didn't miss the piteous looks Justine and Beatrice gave her. Had they figured it out? Surely not! But Edwin had never avoided her that way before. After disappearing the way she did, they surely had put two and two together. They had warned her of the way Edwin worked. They saw it and heard of it before. This was what he did. He used women for what he wanted. After they gave in, he moved on. And Rachael had fallen for every lie out of his mouth, thinking she was somehow different.

She wasn't different. She was just as stupid and gullible as the others.

Her face colored with shame. How they must've talked about her behind her back. They hadn't wanted to protect her as much as they wanted to be proven right. They had been. Edwin was a letch and she was a pitiful fool.

It hadn't been a mistake or oversight on Edwin's part when she saw him at the market with the other woman. He knew she shopped there on Thursday afternoons. He wanted her to see him. He wanted her to be the one to break it off so he wouldn't get his hands dirty. He was clever all right. He would never change his lascivious ways because women like Rachael made it so easy for him.

She cut a slice of bread off the loaf she brought home from Marla's yesterday and nibbled on it. Her stomach instantly settled. Tomorrow morning, she would eat a bite first thing and hopefully avoid the dash to the chamber pot. She carried the bread back to the bed and burrowed under the covers. She wanted to cry. Curse her stupid choices. Beg God to undo the undoable.

She took a tiny bite and sniffed back her tears. A baby. She was going to have a baby. With no husband. The tears spilled over and slid down her cheeks, dampening the bread.

Oh, Lonnie. What would this do to Lonnie? She was quite possibly the worst judge of character on the planet, but she knew he cared for her. Truly cared. He was no Edwin—thank God. Because he wasn't, he would never understand how someone could get into the situation in which she now found herself. How could she—a normally intelligent person—have fallen for a charlatan's charms?

She was going to lose him. He wouldn't want her. The people of Cowboy Creek wouldn't want her in their midst. They were good, honest people. Salt of the earth.

Even if Lonnie was gracious and kind enough to overlook her wretched sin, they never could. They wouldn't want her defiling what they were trying to build here.

Worse, they would look on her child as a...

On her way across the country, she had considered telling everyone she was a widow. Then, if it turned out a baby was coming, they would forgive her. She could explain to Lonnie she hadn't been able to write about her husband in her letters because the pain of losing him was too fresh and too raw.

She even thought up ways to kill off her made-up husband. He had fallen off a dock while unloading freight. He had been killed while rescuing an elderly lady from a runaway grocer's wagon. The burning roof of a foundlings' home crashed in on him while he was rushing the children to safety. Something tragic and heroic that no one could hold against her. She would bask in the love and compassion due a widow and never have to admit her role in her present condition.

As each calamitous scenario formed in her head, she knew immediately she couldn't build an identity on a lie. Whatever happened, she was stuck with the truth. Now the truth was upon her.

How could she have thought for a moment Edwin loved her? Or that she loved him back? Even without Beatrice and Justine's warnings, she had known deep down he was a phony. Everything about him, from the top of his pomaded hair to the soles of his polished loafers, shouted to the world he was a silver-tongued snake who would say or become whatever it took to meet his end, whether in business or in love. Rachael had been swept away by his charisma. She believed she could convert him. Break down his well-manufactured façade.

She laid her hand to her stomach where no swell or tightening of the muscles was yet evident. "I'm sorry, little one, who I allowed to be your father. You deserve a man like Lonnie Fanshaw. A good, kind, honest man who would teach you integrity and fairness."

Her empty stomach cramped from hunger. She needed something more substantial than a piece of bread, but she couldn't bear to sit down at Preach and Marla's table with lies and offense in her belly. She stirred the flames to life in the stove and prepared a cup of tea.

The tea settled her stomach, but it didn't answer any questions about what she was to do or give her the courage to face Lonnie or anyone else. She embarrassed herself yesterday by running away. She had half-expected Lonnie to come after her and demand to know why she kept running every time he got close to her. Part of her wished he would have while the other part wanted to never see him again.

His kiss had made her realize what a fool she'd been over Edwin. It made her accept that she needed to tell him the whole story. Even if she wasn't expecting a child, she couldn't keep the truth from him and hope he never found out. That wouldn't be fair. She had seen in his eyes that he experienced the same spark she did. The same awakening to something that could turn into love. A man couldn't love a woman who wasn't who he thought she was.

At the same time, she couldn't tell him the truth. It would break his heart, and it would break hers for hurting him. She had run. God only knew what he thought, which made the pain that much worse. The only thing she was good for was hurting him.

Oh, Lonnie, what have I done? I don't want to leave, but I don't expect you to want me after this.

She had ruined everything. She threw herself onto the bed and cried herself to sleep.

For three days Rachael stayed in bed, alternately crying and worrying and feeling sorry for herself. If only her mother were here. She would know what to do. She would mop Rachael's feverish brow and pray with her and assure her she was still loved by God and her family. Mama wasn't here. Rachael was alone except for the growing child in her womb, who she was completely unprepared to care for.

She was barely aware of Carrie Whitamore bringing her a mason jar of thin soup on the second day. She looked concerned but didn't press the matter or force herself inside. Carrie may have heard how she rebuffed Lonnie and thought she was suffering from a broken heart, or she was too immature or vain to appreciate the love of a plain man.

Rachael couldn't worry about what Carrie thought. Between her tears and sleep, she hoped Lonnie would come. She didn't know what she'd say to him. Apologize or confess or turn her face to the wall, but she wanted to see him. She missed him.

Oh, she had made such a mess of things.

How had she let this happen? She knew better. She'd been raised better. Her only consolation was her parents weren't here to witness her shame. Their shame.

Deep down, she had known from the beginning that Edwin was a crumb who couldn't be trusted. She had wanted so badly for his words to be true that she ignored the little voice telling her not to give in. She ignored her coworkers' warnings and her own good sense. She wanted to be loved. Cherished. She was dumb enough to believe if she loved him enough, he would change and love her back.

On the third day, a solid knocking sounded at the door. Rachael leaped out of bed in shock. Marla stood at the door with a tray in her hands and her foot outstretched, ready to kick it again if someone didn't answer. She didn't wait for an invitation before pushing past Rachael and inside. She plunked the tray down on the table and pulled off the towel, revealing a bowl of broth and two slices of toast. "I figure this is all you can keep down in the mornings." She set her hands on her wide hips. "Wash up so you can eat and then tell me how long you plan to hide in this house feeling sorry for yourself?"

It took a moment for Rachael to find her voice. The typically jovial, patient Marla reminded her of a bulldog. "How did you know? I barely know myself."

"I suspected it from the day you climbed out of that carriage. You looked a little green and shaky on your feet. I knew it was more than motion sickness."

How mortifying! If Marla figured it out so easily, the other women would too, if they hadn't already. She put her hands over her face but didn't cry. She had no tears left.

She slowly lowered her arms. "Oh, Marla, what have I done?"

Marla patted her back but didn't pull her into the embrace she longed for. "No point in asking questions that don't have answers. Go on now and clean yourself up and eat what I brought you. It's already getting cold."

Woodenly, Rachael moved to the dry sink and brushed out her hair and washed her face and hands. Marla stoked the fire and tidied the table while Rachael worked, neither woman speaking.

Finally, Rachael sat and began to sip at the soup that was only a few degrees warmer than cold. It was still delicious to her empty stomach. Marla sat across from her at the narrow table and rested her chin in her hand. Rachael was afraid to look at her, to see the condemnation, the disgust. She was a scarlet woman. Marla had figured it out. Maybe Carrie too. Soon everyone would know. They would hate her and feel sorry for Lonnie for getting trapped in her web.

The bowl was nearly empty and one piece of limp toast gone before she looked up. "What do I do?"

No judgment showed in Marla's gray eyes. "Tell Lonnie."

Rachael resisted the urge to cover her face again. Telling Lonnie was the last thing she wanted to do. "I don't know if he cares. I haven't seen him since the other day. Since I…"

Since she ran away from him after their kiss. Had he figured it out the same way Marla had? Did he intuitively know she was keeping something from him? Could he also tell by the way she walked, though she doubted men were as observant on those matters as women? She didn't want him to find out any other means than by her telling him, but how could she? He would hate her, if he didn't already.

"I think I'm in love with Lonnie, but I…I ruined everything. He kissed me and I…I ran away. Now, with this, what difference does it make? No man will want a woman who…" A small sob burst from her throat. "A woman who's done what I've done."

Marla rested her hand on Rachael's arm. "You're calling a whole lot of things into being that haven't happened yet. You came here to marry Lonnie. You think you love him, which from my experience, means you do. I can tell he loves you. All I've heard so far is you feeling sorry for yourself. I understand it, but I'm not going to sit here and let you hurt Lonnie because you can't face what's happened. You're here and a baby's coming. Neither of those things can be changed at this moment. Regardless of whether the two of you wind up together or not, he deserves the truth. You can't disappear into the night if that's what you're thinking of doing."

Rachael shook her head in despair. "I'm not thinking of anything. I can't think. I don't know what to do."

Marla frowned and didn't speak for a minute. At length, she gently patted Rachael's arm, but her expression didn't change. "First and foremost, you need to talk this over with the good Lord if you haven't already. You need to confess your sins. Your fears and doubts, even though He already knows it all. Then you're going to talk to Lonnie. Whatever happens will happen. Eventually, like it or not, everyone in Cowboy Creek is going to know. It isn't fair that Lonnie doesn't find out first."

Rachael dropped her head into her hands. Marla was right, but how would she do any of it?

Marla took hold of her shoulder and pulled her upright. "Do you want to marry Lonnie?" Her voice and face were hard.

Rachael opened her mouth but closed it as she thought for a moment. She wouldn't answer rashly. She dried her face with her hands. "I think so. Yes, I do."

Marla let go of her and stood. She dried her own hands on her apron. "Then you're going to have to finish your soup and figure this out. Regardless of whatever you do or don't do, you're having a baby, God willing." She glanced at Rachael's midsection as if she were seeing right through it. "No matter how it came about, a little one is coming into the world. A being that was wonderfully and fearfully made by the Maker of the stars. You need to get yourself ready to be its mama."

Chapter Twelve

After Marla left, Rachael felt like crying some more, but she couldn't take one more minute of self-loathing. Marla was right; a baby was coming. Regardless of what Lonnie decided to do about the matter, she was going to be a mama. Time to stop thinking of herself and start thinking of what her baby needed. No matter how she felt or her level of humiliation and self-pity, she couldn't lie in bed with the covers over her head for the rest of her life, though that's exactly what she wanted to do. Her actions would bring Lonnie embarrassment and pain. She wouldn't add to it by letting him hear rumors and innuendo. She owed it to her unborn child to get up and get her blood flowing. She heated water and took a bath and washed her hair. That alone made her feel better than she had in days.

She stepped outside into the fresh air and breathed deeply. The last few days had been gray and dreary with heavy clouds spitting frozen snow against her windowpane. Today the sun shone brightly as if in agreement with Marla that it was time she stop hiding from what she'd done.

Her feet turned in the direction of the stream with no thought on her part. Halfway there, she realized she was walking the same path Lonnie had taken her the other night. No matter what decision she made, she owed him the truth. She couldn't for the life of her figure out how to tell him. How did one bring it up in conversation?

"Lovely day, isn't it? Oh, and by the way, I'm going to have a baby. I apologize for any pain or embarrassment it might cause you, but I thought you should know."

He would hate her. Everyone in Cowboy Creek would hate her, but no more than she hated herself. They liked and respected Lonnie. That she had come with a plan to saddle him with another man's child would turn their stomachs as it should.

The rush of water grew louder, drowning out her thoughts. She focused on the sound and the glint of sunlight off the water through the bare trees. Water had always calmed her. Her neighborhood back home had not been one of the best, but from a park on a hillside, she could sit and watch the grand Ohio River rushing by. There were benches and meandering trails, always crowded with children and strolling couples, young and old. Rachael often carried a book in her bag, More often than not, she would end up watching the crowds without opening her book and wonder about their stories.

Which couples were in love? Which children were happy and content and living the life she dreamed of giving her own children someday?

The water always soothed her and reminded her she wasn't alone. God was in control of the river and the river's source. He was equally qualified to look after her. Her foot slipped on the wet rocks. A small cry escaped her lips as she righted herself. She shouldn't go any farther. She wasn't fond of falling. Now that she was carrying a child, it was even more foolhardy.

Heavy footfalls sounded above her on the rocks. "Rachael?"

She turned and looked up toward the voice. She spotted him through the trees. Dread and hope filled her heart. "Lonnie. Here." She waved. He caught sight of her and picked his way down the hillside to where she stood. "I heard you cry out. Are you all right?"

Hope surged in her chest. He cared for her, even after the other day. Maybe he could forgive her. As soon as the thought occurred to her, she knew it was a fool's dream. "I slipped. I didn't realize I cried out so loud."

"You didn't. Sound just travels easily here. What are you doing down here by yourself?"

"I needed to think."

He gave her a long look. "About what has kept you holed up in the brides' house the past three days?"

Rachael's blood ran cold. Did he already know? She hoped not, though she had no idea how to tell him.

"I guess you know there's something I need to tell you."

He looked past her toward the water. "I figured as much."

She twisted her hands together. "I'm sorry, Lonnie. I don't know how to say it. It's…"

He brought his gaze back to her. "You don't need to agonize over it so much. I've been around a long time. I know how the world works. What a woman wants. I was a fool to think you'd settle for me anyway. For this place."

"What? No."

"I like you, Rachael. A lot. But I won't beg. I don't want a woman who doesn't want me back. Me and the other fellas discussed it when we sent for brides. If a woman didn't want to stay, for whatever reason, we'd pay her fare back home or wherever else she wanted to go. We planned to split the costs evenly, but that isn't fair to the rest of them, especially now that they have brides. You're my responsibility. I'll pay your fare myself. I can give you a little extra for expenses to set yourself up."

"Lonnie, stop! That's not what I'm saying."

He wagged his head. "It's all right. It happens. Not everybody makes a good match. I don't want you to feel bad about it. I know what women see when they look at me."

"Lonnie! I'm going to have a baby!"

"What?"

"I'm going to have a baby," she repeated, her voice small and broken.

His jaw went slack. His eyes widened. He worked his jaw a time or two before any sound came out. "I don't...I...uh...didn't know there was another man. I thought—"

"There was a man, but it isn't what you think."

His eyes went dark. His large fists clenched and unclenched. She could see the direction his mind was going. "He didn't hurt me, Lonnie." she said quickly to diffuse his fury at a man he'd never met. "It wasn't like that."

His lips went flat, and he glared down at her. "Then what was it like?"

Rachael's stomach tightened. The blood drained from her face. Even if he hated her, he deserved the whole story, not a whitewashed version that made her look like a victim who hadn't known what she was doing. She had willfully chosen to look past Edwin's faults to satisfy her desperate desire for love and validation. She couldn't keep blaming him for what happened between them.

"I thought I loved him. No, I *wanted* to love him. I wanted a man who was sophisticated and refined."

He seemed to withdraw into himself. "Someone unlike me."

"Yes. I mean no. I thought he was what I wanted. I had a picture of what I wanted my life to look like. I wanted to open my own shop. I wanted to see women all over the city wearing hats I designed. I thought he had the same vision. I thought we would—"

She stopped talking. "None of that matters. All that matters is I sinned against God. And myself. And you." She squeezed her eyes shut, trying to organize the thoughts crashing around in her head.

"I should've told you before I came. I should've told Miss Canfield. If I had, she wouldn't have let me come, and I wouldn't have met you and put you into the middle of something you didn't ask for."

She resisted the urge to touch him. The look on his face, the rigidity in his shoulders, told her a touch was not welcome. She wanted to explain why she'd fallen for Edwin. The emptiness and insecurity inside her that drew her to a man who seemed to fill any room he walked into. But she wouldn't manipulate him by trying to garner sympathy. She would accept her role without resorting to poor-me excuses.

"After coming here, after meeting you, I learned what a real man is. It wasn't him. I was a fool to think he was. Even a bigger fool for having dragged you into this by…by falling in love with you."

Her heart lurched. She had told Marla she thought she loved him. Now she knew she did. More than she thought possible to love anyone. She hadn't thought of love until this moment. She loved Lonnie, which made her despise her selfishness that much more.

He was staring at her as if trying to decide if she was sincere or telling him what she thought he wanted to hear.

He cared for her. He might even love her back. She suspected she had in her feminine arsenal the words to get through to him—the words that would get her way to a man enamored with her. But she wouldn't use them. She had run from Cincinnati so she wouldn't have to face the people in Mr. Winegard's shop. She was a coward. She wouldn't be a coward with Lonnie. He could send her away if he wanted, but she wouldn't leave with regrets. With words on her heart she didn't have the nerve to say.

She silently prayed for strength to get it out before she lost her nerve or he shut her off. "I've only been here a few weeks, but I feel like a completely different person than I was in Cincinnati. I think it's because of you. You're everything that other man was not. You're caring and kind and honest. Most of all, you're genuine. You don't pretend to be something you're not to impress people."

His eyes were dark and unreadable. If only she could tell what he was thinking. She wished he'd say something. Anything. Even if he told her to get out of his face and he never wanted to see her again. At least then, she'd know.

"I never meant to hurt you. I can't undo any of this situation." She looked across the sparkling water to the other side of the stream she'd never been to. "Ever since I left Cincinnati—before that, even—I've done nothing but feel sorry for myself. Now, I don't know if I would undo any of it, even if I could."

She looked back at him. "It sounds crazy, and I've created a terrible predicament for myself, but I think I love my baby. I think I'm looking forward to meeting her...or him. I may have lost every friend I have. The women here may not want to see my face after they find out what kind of person I am." Tears clouded her vision. "I may have lost you."

He looked toward the trees and ran his hand through his thinning hair. His profile was intense and brooding. He stared at everything but her.

"Lonnie?" She bit back the plaintiveness in her voice. She didn't want him to feel sorry for her, to make a decision out of pity. She only wanted a man who would love her. "Say something. Tell me what you're thinking. Even if I won't want to hear it."

After a long moment, he looked at her. "I don't know what I'm thinking. I only know I can't talk to anyone right now." He looked down at her black boots on the rocks. "Will you be all right? Can you get back to the road by yourself?"

She nearly burst into tears. Even after learning the evil she'd done, his first concern was her safety. "Yes," she murmured.

He nodded, let out a long sigh, and turned and walked away. Rachael stared after him. She thought of watching Edwin walk away after he told her he wouldn't change his life for any woman. He liked her, but he liked his freedom and independence more. At the time, Rachael thought her heart would break wide open. Deep down, she had known it wasn't Edwin she mourned, but the humiliation she would face when the girls at work found out he dumped her after they warned her that he was a rogue and a user.

She had never loved Edwin. She convinced herself she had because he was everything she thought she wanted. Now she realized the only thing she wanted was walking away from her up the hill.

Chapter Thirteen

Rachael didn't cry when she got back to the brides' house. She had no right to. Everything she was going through she'd brought on herself. Her mind whirled as she tried to figure out what to do. She still had a little money. Very little, but maybe enough to start earning a living for herself and the baby. She thought of the woman in Good Hope who Lonnie said might fix her cloak. Perhaps she could talk the woman into hiring her and they could open a shop. Good Hope didn't look like it was big enough to support such a business but maybe it looked that way because no one had ever tried. Rachael knew sales. She would convince the woman they could make and sell things besides dresses and hats. They could make men's and children's clothing. Tablecloths. Quilts. Whatever she could think of that required a little creativity and a needle and thread.

If the woman in Good Hope wasn't interested or the market wasn't big enough to support such an endeavor, she would move to the next town. Ruby City sounded feasible. Or she'd go all the way to Denver.

But, oh, she didn't want to do that. She didn't want to leave Lonnie.

Whatever happened, she had peace about the situation. God would work it out. She was carrying a child. According to the Bible, every child was a gift from God. She may not have chosen her gift to come about the way it did, but it was a gift nonetheless. A gift she would cherish and honor and raise in a way that pleased God.

For the first time in several days, she had an appetite. She still had the jar of soup Carrie Whitamore had brought over. She dumped it into a small pot and put it on the stove. While it heated, she took her Bible off the bedside table. She hadn't been able to focus on the message for days, but today she would.

After she ate, she tidied the cabin, then read some more. She wasn't going to spend the next few months worrying about what she would do and how she would survive with a child. The baby was coming; there was nothing she could do about that. She would work hard and accept what happened, but the details she would have to leave to God. She saw no way out of the situation. No light at the end of the tunnel. She would put her faith in God and trust that however He worked out the situation would be for her good.

She nearly gave in to self-pity every time Lonnie flashed across her mind. The thought of never seeing him again was crushing. Funny that her biggest concern when Edwin walked away was what others would think of her.

The shadow on the wall moved toward evening. She was hungry again. A good appetite was a good sign. Perhaps she was over the sickness that plagued her the last few weeks. She would go to Marla's and help with preparations for the evening meal. Her stomach tightened. She hadn't seen Preach in days. Marla had surely told him why Rachael hadn't come out of the brides' house. She dreaded what he must think of her, but she couldn't let her pride stop her from living. She'd spent enough time hiding. Time she became a help to these kind people until she moved on.

She swung open the door. Her heart leapt in her throat. Lonnie stood on the other side. "Lonnie. You startled me."

"I didn't mean to." He raised his arm. Draped over it was her cloak. "I wanted to bring this back."

Rachael's heart sank. Now there was nothing keeping her here. Then she noticed it was clean as new and back to forest green. "What did you do?"

"I took it to Good Hope the other day."

"I wish you hadn't bothered."

"I told you I would. It was my fault it got covered in ash. I caught Mrs. Gowdy on a good day. She had time to work on it." He unfolded it, gave it a gentle shake to remove the wrinkles, and held it up for her perusal. "Looks right as rain to me. I never dreamed she'd get the soot out. Got the smell out too." He lowered his nose to the fabric and sniffed.

Rachael couldn't keep from smiling. "Oh, Lonnie, you're so kind. You didn't need to go to all that trouble but thank you. It means a lot. I…" Tears filled her eyes. She swallowed hard. She wouldn't give in to them. She'd cried enough over her mistakes.

She reached for the cloak. Lonnie kept hold of it. "Could I come in? I'd like to talk if you don't mind."

Rachael realized the temperature had dropped with the setting sun. Cold air filled the little house. "Yes, of course." She backed inside. Lonnie was too polite to walk away from her without an explanation the way he'd done at the creek. He would tell her what was on his heart, just like she had wanted to do with him.

He closed the door without taking his eyes off her. He handed her the cloak. She hung it on the coatrack he made for her. Her fingers stroked the cool metal as she gently hung the cape. He cared for her so much. She would always carry that in her heart. Her only regret was the child she carried wasn't his.

When she turned, she found him watching her. She was thankful he hadn't shoved the cloak at her and stormed back to the smithy.

He took off his hat and turned it round and round in his hands. "I shouldn't have taken off like I did last night. I…I needed to think." He looked directly into her eyes, his expression earnest. "All afternoon I've been thinking about raising another man's child. Sometimes God calls us to do things we never thought we'd do."

Rachael's breath caught in her throat.

He set his hat on the table and took a deep breath as if he was struggling with the situation as much as she was. "All afternoon I puttered around the shop, trying to accomplish something and doing nothing but getting in my own way. All I could think on was how empty the place was without you. Without you at the table sharing a meal. Trying to outdo me in the kitchen."

His lips twitched. He dragged his hand through his hair. His unruly cowlick made his head look lopsided. She nearly smiled.

"I don't know what the future will bring," he said. "I can't imagine anything beyond this moment. All I know is I don't want to go back to that empty house without you. Back to the life I had before you came."

Her brow furrowed. Should she hope he was saying what she thought he was saying?

He lunged forward and grabbed her arms. He pulled her against him and lowered his mouth to hers. He let go and encircled her with his muscled arms, pulling her even closer. Rachael slid her arms around his neck and clung to him.

When they drew apart, he leaned back and gazed into her eyes. "There it is," he whispered.

"There what is?" Her voice was hoarse and clogged with tears.

"What I waited for my whole life."

"I don't—"

He cut her off. "I love you, Rachael. I have since the moment you stepped off that stage. I know it's crazy. I know you can't love somebody just by looking at her. But I did. It's like God told me after all those months of waiting—all those times I saw brides ride into town and choose someone else—that you were here, and you were the one He sent just for me." He squeezed her tighter. "I had to wait for the look to confirm it."

She laughed at the intensity on his face. "What look?"

"The one you're wearing right now. The look that says you're not disappointed."

"Oh, Lonnie, I could never be disappointed—"

He kissed her again, cutting off her words, then rested his forehead against hers. "I'm so glad you're here, Rachael Zeldin. You having a baby doesn't change that. Nothing ever will. You're going to have a baby, and it's going to be *our* baby. And that's all right with me cause God sent you. Who am I to argue with His plan?"

"Lonnie. You're too good to me. How can I ever make it up to you?"

"Just keep looking at me the way you're looking at me now. The way Ma always looked at Pa."

She still had no idea what he was talking about, but it didn't matter. She tightened her arms around his neck and gave in to tears of joy.

❀ ❀ ❀

Marla smoothed the jacket down over the back of Rachael's skirt. "Sorry, honey. Looks like you've put on a little weight. I'll have to keep two of these buttons unfastened. Don't worry, your jacket covers it."

Rachael put her hands to her flaming cheeks. "Oh, Marla, I still can't believe my wedding day is happening like this." She turned away from the mirror. "What's everyone going to think?"

"They're going to think you're beautiful and they never saw Lonnie looking happier. They'll probably clap and cheer and embarrass the life out of you."

"It won't take long for them to figure out there's a baby coming…if they haven't already." Tears clouded her eyes. "I don't care what they think of me. I just don't want them thinking less of Lonnie."

"Stop that crying. You'll get your face all splotchy. Lonnie can take care of himself. But let me tell you right now those people won't think anything. If they do, well, that's between them and God. We've all sinned, Rachael. The only difference between the rest of us and you is you have to wear your sin where everybody can see it. As soon as you ask for forgiveness with a contrite heart, God freely gives it. He doesn't keep an account, so no one else has the right to either. He loves you. Lonnie loves you. And that darling little baby you're carrying is gonna love you."

"Oh, Marla, what would I do without you?"

"That's what I wonder every time one of you brides come riding in on the stage."

Rachael laughed. Marla laughed back. She pulled a handkerchief out of her sleeve and dabbed the end of Rachael's nose. "There, that's better. That's the face Lonnie is waiting to see. We don't want to put a damper on the day by presenting him with a bride with a red nose."

They turned toward the door where Rachael's bags and trunks were packed and waiting. She'd only lived in this small house for a month, yet it felt like the most important parts of her life had happened here. "Should I ask Lonnie to take my things up to the house before meeting?"

"No need. Some of the men will take them up while you're enjoying your cake. Now let's get to the church. I'm getting pretty good at the wedding march if I do say so myself. I can't wait to do it one more time."

Lonnie was waiting at the door when Rachael stepped outside. Marla came out behind her, still fussing with Rachael's hair.

"Everybody's in the meetinghouse waiting."

A blush crept up her cheeks. Her heart swelled at the sight of him. She didn't want to have a red nose during her wedding ceremony, but it seemed like all she wanted to do was cry these days. This time, though, they were tears of happiness. She never thought a man would have her after what happened between her and Edwin.

Lonnie Fanshaw was like no man she ever met.

"I'm sorry you had to wait."

He chuckled and tucked her hand in the crook of his elbow. "All I've done is wait for you for the last forty years. What's a few more minutes?"

She couldn't hold back her tears. It looked like Lonnie was going to marry a bride with a red nose after all. He took her hand and walked her across the street. It was another cold, dreary November day, but this time she didn't mind. No longer did she find the streets bleak and the landscape barren. Lonnie tightened his hold on her arm. She looked into his eyes. She wanted to kiss him, but she was aware of Marla walking behind her and the rest of Cowboy Creek waiting at the meetinghouse. There'd be plenty of time for kisses later. Her cheeks warmed in anticipation.

The sound of an approaching rig reached their ears. Marla shaded her eyes with her hand. "I thought you said everyone was already here," she told Lonnie.

"They are. Can't imagine who it might be."

Marla gasped. "New neighbors! Do you think? The last time Daniel was in Good Hope, he heard rumblings that folks might be moving out this way."

They picked up their pace across the street. Lonnie squeezed Rachael's hand. "Would you look at that."

A team of two roan horses drove into view. A tall, finely outfitted surrey wagon was driven by a man in a dark suit and derby hat. "Oh, my," Rachael said. "And on a Sunday no less."

Across the road Jacob Campbell and Nathan Lake were about to go inside the meetinghouse. They turned and stared for a moment before coming back down the stairs. Everyone inside must've heard the surrey, too, for the building quickly emptied. Jacob hurried back up the steps to take his wife's hand. According to Marla, Rennie's baby was due to make an appearance by the end of the year. Rachael smiled to herself, knowing she would look like Rennie by Spring.

J.T. Whitamore burst through the crowd and ran into the street. "It's people. People's coming."

"J.T., get out of the way," his mother chastened.

He looked at her over his shoulder without moving from the middle of the road. "I hope they got a boy. Please, let 'em have a boy," he called to the sky.

Everyone laughed as they moved into the road, elbowing each other and speculating. "I can't imagine a family riding all this way in a surrey," someone said.

"With a hired driver, it looks like," someone else said.

Rachael put her hand on Lonnie's shoulder for balance and climbed onto the base of the pump. She craned her neck to see. The driver was definitely a hired man wearing a navy blue uniform with shiny brass buttons. The wagon drew closer, and she got a full view of the woman over the driver's shoulder. She gasped and stretched higher to make sure her eyes weren't deceiving her.

"It's Nan!" she shrieked. "Nan Canfield, Rase's aunt." She squeezed Lonnie's shoulder. He swung her to the ground. She ran into the street with J.T.

"It's Nan," she told the other women.

"Nan?" they said in unison and began to push forward. Rase Canfield stepped out of the crowd as the wagon clattered to a stop in the now blocked road. In her excitement, Rachael elbowed past him. "Nan! It's me, Rachael."

Nan's face erupted into a wide smile. "Rachael. Oh, dear heart. I'm so happy to see you. How lovely to see all of you." She stood in the surrey and reached for Rase's hand. "I apologize for traveling on the Lord's Day, but a washed out bridge prevented us from arriving yesterday. There was nowhere for us to stay over so we decided to forsake propriety and come anyway."

Rachael wondered briefly who she meant by *we*, but she was too excited for questions. "You couldn't have better timing. Today's my wedding day." She glanced around for Lonnie and found him standing directly behind her. She grabbed his hand. "We're getting married."

Nan clasped her free hand over her bosom. "Oh, that's just what I wanted to hear. Rase, dear, help me out of this thing so this young woman can marry her groom."

Rase said something Rachael couldn't hear and took both her hands and helped her out of the surrey. It was then Rachael spotted a woman a few years younger than herself nestled under a mountain of blankets. The other brides noticed, too, and pressed in close for an explanation from Nan.

"Looks like there's going to be trouble," Lonnie said into Rachael's ear, his breath deliciously warm on her face. He wagged his head at Rase, who was glowering at his aunt.

Rachael stifled a giggle behind her gloved hand. Rase didn't stand a chance. If Nan believed her nephew needed a bride, then a bride he would get.

She leaned into Lonnie's chest. She'd wonder about Rase and the woman in the surrey some other time. All she could think about now was getting into the meetinghouse and marrying the man she loved.

The *only* man. In spite of her sin, in spite of her vanity and mistakes, God had led her to Cowboy Creek and given her and her child the man she didn't know they needed. The woman who arranged it all had arrived just in time to share her blessed day. God was truly a God of mercy and miracles.

The End

Before You Go

If you enjoyed Scarlett and Rachael's stories, please leave a review on Amazon or any other marketplace or blog that allows reviews. Even a short review proves to Amazon there is interest in the book, and they will display it to more readers and more people can learn about the *Nine Brides Series*.

The best way to support an author is still the old-fashioned method of recommending books to a friend. Share any of my links on social media outlets. Follow me on Amazon, BookBub and GoodReads. Give the books a thumbs up and leave a comment whenever you see them posted somewhere. No greater compliment can be paid to any author of stories you love.

I love hearing from readers. Email me at teresa@teresaslack.com anytime with your thoughts and input about my stories and series ideas you would love to read.

Read for Free

Sign up for my newsletter and receive a free download of A Promise for Josie: A Willow Wood Brides Prequel

After a broken promise and a broken heart, is love worth the risk?

Abandoned at the altar on her wedding day, Josie Segal doubts she'll ever find true love. When a tall stranger rides into Josie's life, her dreams of love and adventure are reawakened. Can she move beyond the pain and fear of broken promises to trust Owen Dutton, and her own heart?

About the Author

Teresa Slack loves reading, writing, and falling in love. Creating clean and wholesome western romances where cowboys still sweep independent women off their feet was an easy choice for her.

She writes from her home in the beautiful southern Ohio hills, which she shares with her husband and rescue dog and rescue cats. Any errors and typos she blames on the cats, randomly running across her keyboard.